"We don't even know each other."

Ilya's arm slipped around Yasmin's waist and he stepped in closer. "I think we can produce a reasonable facsimile, don't you?"

He lowered his face to hers, his lips hovering a mere hairbreadth away from her mouth. She could see the silver striations that radiated from his pupils and the rim of dark blue around his irises. He really had the most beautiful eyes she'd ever seen.

His hand was strong against her back. Supporting. Warm. The warmth spread through her dress and seeped slowly into her skin.

A shiver ran up her back in total contrast.

He might essentially be a stranger to her, but he affected her on a level that both intrigued and frightened her at the same time.

* * *

Tangled Vows is part of the Marriage at First Sight series from *USA TODAY* bestselling author Yvonne Lindsay!

Dear Reader,

Are you a reality TV fan? I admit, from time to time I get caught up in whatever the latest trend is, but the shows usually fail to hold my attention for longer than a couple of episodes. The latest round of meet-and-marry-at-the-altar type shows did get my creative juices flowing, though, and when I pitched the idea for a series on this theme, with a few differences, I was thrilled to get the go-ahead. It hasn't been as easy as I thought to write these stories, I have to say, because I guess in fiction, as in real life, there are certain rules that can't be broken and situations that simply don't occur.

So, here we have *Tangled Vows*. Ilya and Yasmin's journey to love is anything but smooth, and all the way through I found myself asking if a match made in marriage could really lead to a forever love for these two strong-minded and independent individuals. But, as my mother always says, there's a lid for every pot, and these two were meant to be together, even if it takes a while to find that particular "fit."

I do hope you enjoy reading how they overcome their trials and tribulations to their happy-ever-after and that you'll continue to enjoy my Marriage at First Sight series. As always, I love hearing from my readers. You can contact me through my website, www.yvonnelindsay.com, or my Facebook page, www.Facebook.com/yvonnelindsayauthor.

Happy reading!

Yvonne Lindsay

YVONNE LINDSAY

TANGLED VOWS

Recycling programs
for this product may
not exist in your area.

ISBN-13: 978-1-335-97158-6

Tangled Vows

This edition published by arrangement with Harlequin Books S.A.

For questions and comments about the quality of this book, please contact us at CustomerService@Harlequin.com.

Printed in U.S.A.

A typical Piscean, *USA TODAY* bestselling author **Yvonne Lindsay** has always preferred her imagination to the real world. Married to her blind-date hero and with two adult children, she spends her days crafting the stories of her heart, and in her spare time she can be found with her nose in a book reliving the power of love, or knitting socks and daydreaming. Contact her via her website, yvonnelindsay.com.

Books by Yvonne Lindsay

Harlequin Desire

Wed at Any Price

Honor-Bound Groom
Stand-In Bride's Seduction
For the Sake of the Secret Child

Courtesan Brides

Arranged Marriage, Bedroom Secrets
Contract Wedding, Expectant Bride

Marriage at First Sight

Tangled Vows

Visit her Author Profile page at Harlequin.com, or yvonnelindsay.com, for more titles.

To the awesome team at Harlequin who shine my ideas and my words to a high polish and who dream up titles when I cannot and who create amazing covers for my readers to love and who take care of all the behind-the-scenes stuff I don't even know about—thank you. I wouldn't be where I am without you all.

One

"There's been a terrible mistake."

Yasmin Carter froze—poised in her wedding finery at the end of the royal blue carpet leading to the altar. She stared at the man who had just turned to face her. Ilya Horvath, heir apparent to the Horvath empire, CEO of her biggest business rival.

Her groom. The one she was meeting for the first time today.

Her eyes skimmed the small gathering of guests flanking the aisle. Their expressions registered varying degrees of dismay and shock at her words. She forced her gaze back toward Ilya. He did not look surprised…or amused. In fact, he looked annoyed.

Well, that was fine with her. She was pretty annoyed, too, right now, and she'd tell the Match Made in Marriage people at the first opportunity. When her office manager, Riya, had brought the matchmaking business to her attention, it had appeared to be a solution to her current business woes. Cost aside, she had stood to gain more if she went through the type of arranged marriage at first sight offered by Match Made in Marriage than if she remained single. She'd endured the psychometric testing and the interviews with the end goal in mind—securing an exclusive deal to handle Hardacre Incorporated's corporate and family travel for the next five years. The company was a well-known motivational and business coaching enterprise that worked all over the country. That agreement was the golden treasure that would pull her small charter airline out of the red and back into the black—so she'd signed the detailed contract that stipulated she must stay married to her stranger-husband for at least three months without a second thought. But contract or no contract, this wedding simply could not happen.

She should never have entered into this ridiculous scheme to save her business, but her inside source had warned her that the owner's wife would never allow her husband to do business on a regular basis with a beautiful, young, unmarried woman. Wallace Hardacre had a wandering eye but was known to leave married women alone.

It had seemed so simple. To seal the deal, she needed to be married. She knew she had everyone else's quotes beaten on price. And it wasn't as if she didn't want to marry Mr. Right someday. She absolutely did. It was just that with running the company and all the hours that took, she didn't have time to form quality relationships with men.

Her gaze caught and meshed with Ilya's for just a moment and a shiver ran through her. Not of apprehension, exactly—something more primitive than that. But it was enough for her to be certain that this whole thing had been a mistake from the start.

Ilya Horvath might look as though he'd stepped from the pages of *GQ* but there was no way she could consider marrying him.

Physically, of course, he was perfect. Tall, with broad shoulders filling out his suit to perfection and a light beard wreathing his jaw, he was—in a word—gorgeous. Attraction rippled through Yasmin's body, making the corset beneath her strapless bodice suddenly feel a hundred times tighter than when Riya had hooked her into it this morning. Yasmin clamped down on the sensation and forced herself to take a breath, reminding herself that mentally, emotionally, socially and fiscally he was all wrong for her. No, she couldn't do this to her late granddad's memory—not to the man who'd taken her in and raised her when her parents had dumped her on him so they could continue to pursue their adventures rather than face up to adulthood and responsibility. She couldn't marry the man whose own grandfather, her granddad's best friend, had stolen and married the woman her grandfather loved. Attraction was all very well and good, but not when two families had been feuding for as long as theirs had.

"There's definitely been a mistake," she repeated, more firmly this time.

She bent and gathered the fullness of her layered organza gown, completed a swift one-eighty and exited the ballroom as fast as her feet, clad in intricately beaded slippers, would carry her. There was total silence for a few seconds, then the room broke out in a clatter of noise that followed her down the wide corridor.

Yasmin didn't know which way to go as she headed into the resort's foyer. To the elevators and back to the luxurious honeymoon suite where she'd gotten ready this morning or straight out the front door and hope there was a cab waiting there? It was a long way from here in Port Ludlow, Washington, to her home in California. The fare would be—

"Yasmin!" a woman called from behind her. "Please, wait. We need to talk."

Yasmin turned to face the petite, elegant older woman now approaching her. Alice Horvath—the woman responsible for the bitter rivalry between the Carters and the Horvaths these past sixty-plus years.

"There's nothing you can say that will make me change my mind," Yasmin said firmly.

"Just give me a moment of your time." Alice put a gentle hand on Yasmin's arm. "Please? It's important."

"Look, I—"

"Perhaps up in your suite would be best, more private." Alice began to steer Yasmin toward the elevators.

The adrenaline that had surged through Yasmin's

body at the sight of her intended groom began to abate, leaving a dragging lethargy in its wake.

"Fine, but you, of all people, should know you're wasting your time if you're going to try and persuade me to marry your grandson."

The older woman gave her a sweet smile in response but said nothing as they rode the elevator up to the honeymoon suite. Yasmin was surprised when Alice produced a key card that opened the door.

"Forgive me the intrusion," Alice said, closing the door behind them. "I was merely holding the key for Ilya until after the ceremony."

Yasmin didn't know what to say or where to look, so she opted to plunk herself down on one of the sofas in the sitting room. Alice gracefully seated herself opposite.

"You have a right to know what's going on."

Damn right she did. Yasmin tightly squeezed the bound stems of her bouquet of pale pink roses and gypsophila to stop the trembling that had begun in her fingers and now threatened to travel up her arms and take over her entire body.

"Let me be frank with you, my dear. When you applied to Match Made in Marriage I immediately knew you and my grandson were compatible. I didn't need the specialist tests to assure me that you and Ilya would very much be a perfect match."

"I beg your pardon? You work with Match Made in Marriage? Are you telling me that *you* make the matches?" Yasmin replied in stunned surprise.

"It's not widely known, of course, and we do take

the tests and interviews into consideration, but more as a confirmation that I'm on the right track with my couples. Trust me when I say I've always had a knack for these things. Once I retired from the family firm it was purely common sense to turn my little talent into a business. When my grandson told me he was ready to marry and settle down, it was only natural he would turn to me, but I didn't expect to find the perfect match for him so promptly. I have to say, getting your application was quite the surprise."

Alice Horvath looked at the beautiful but clearly confused and angry young woman sitting opposite her and wished things could have been different between their families. That the painful rift between best friends hadn't formed when Jim Carter and Eduard Horvath both fell in love with her and, eventually, fallen out forever when she chose Eduard for her husband. But this was her chance to make things right—to heal the wounds of so long ago and to put this stupid feud to bed once and for all.

If only she could persuade Yasmin to go ahead with the wedding.

She drew in a breath and chose her words carefully. If there was anything this young woman seemed to have a grasp of, it was business. Oh, yes, Alice knew that Carter Air was struggling. She also knew that Yasmin, despite having come up with the hefty commitment fee, could not afford to break the terms of the marriage contract she'd signed or attempt to sue Match Made in Marriage to get out of it.

Alice sighed softly and composed herself.

"I repeat, matching you and Ilya is no mistake. The two of you are perfectly suited to each other and are fully compatible when it comes to your values and your hopes and dreams for the future. I have every faith that you belong together and that you could make a long and very satisfying marriage."

"But—"

Alice raised a hand. "Please, allow me to finish. There comes a time when the past has to be put behind us so we can look to the future. This is your time. I know that there's been a great deal of bitterness between our families, that your grandfather and my Eduard ceased to have a civil word to say to each other after..." Alice blinked away the emotion, the weakness she couldn't afford to show. "Suffice it to say that bitterness has tainted too many lives for far too long."

"It's not just a family feud, Mrs. Horvath—"

"Please, call me Alice," she interrupted. "And, yes, I know it goes deeper than that. But I urge you to reconsider and to return to the ceremony. Everyone is waiting."

"I can't do it. I can't go against everything I've ever been raised to believe. I can't marry the man whose business is trying to put *me* out of business. I owe it to my staff and to my grandfather's memory to walk away from this. I want to invoke the exit clause in my contract early. Ilya and I are incompatible on far too many levels."

Yasmin's gray eyes flashed with emotion, reminding Alice so much of Yasmin's grandfather.

"Ah, my dear. So often pride comes before a fall. Your beloved grandfather aside, you owe it to your staff to go through with this. Let's be honest. You're not in the best position financially, are you?" Alice paused to let her words sink in. To ensure that Yasmin was aware that she knew exactly what the younger woman's situation was right now. "The figures you provided as proof of your monetary position were inflated, to put it kindly, and before you ask, yes, we checked."

Yasmin began to protest but Alice cut her off.

"You gave us every right to examine your financial situation when you signed the contract. Let's be quite honest with each other. We both know you can most certainly do without the negative public fallout of walking away from your contractual obligations, not to mention the financial fallout from attempting to break your contract with Match Made in Marriage. I know you took out a loan to fund your application. A loan secured by the assets of Carter Air, I believe?"

She watched Yasmin grow pale as her words sank in.

"You're threatening me with ruin? Really? All to *make* me marry your grandson?"

"Sometimes, my girl, the ends justify the means. Don't you think your future happiness is worth it?"

"So you want me, specifically, to marry Ilya. Why?"

Alice studied Yasmin, her ashen face, her clear gray eyes, the set of her pretty mouth and the proud posture as she fought a battle she couldn't win. She recognized the girl's spirit; after all, hadn't she been just such a young woman once? And Alice was no different now. She still fought hard for what was best for everyone she loved. This was important and she was convinced, beyond a doubt, that Ilya and Yasmin belonged together. She wouldn't have made this match if she hadn't known, deep in her bones, that they were right for each other. That "knack" she'd mentioned earlier—it had manifested early in her life. A knowing that some might call mumbo jumbo and others prescience. Whatever it was, it was her gift and she only used her gift for good.

Alice loved her eldest grandson, the son of her first-born son, more fiercely than she'd ever believed possible. This woman was the key to his long-term happiness—she knew it as surely as she knew she'd made the right decision when she'd chosen Eduard Horvath for her husband. As surely as she'd known every one of the matches she'd engineered was right. She only hoped Yasmin would come to see that, too.

"I love my grandson dearly, but he works too hard and, deep down, I don't believe he's happy. You, whether you realize it or not, hold the key to his future happiness. I wish nothing more than to see him and his bride happy together. It's as simple—and as complicated—as that." Alice flicked an invisible speck of dust off the sleeve of her impeccably tailored jacket. "Now, shall we return? We both know you can't afford not to let this wedding go ahead."

"But what about the clear conflict of interest? Ilya is my business rival. How are we to manage that?"

"That is something you will need to work out together."

"No, that's not enough for me. I need to know that the Horvaths will not interfere with Carter Air. Ilya's company has either bought or driven out of business every other small charter company at the airfield. I will not let that happen to Carter Air. I made a promise to my grandfather that I would keep his legacy safe."

Alice nodded and gave Yasmin a small smile of compassion. "Dear girl, I know you loved your grandfather dearly. For all his bluster and noise, he was a man who cared deeply. But sometimes promises made in the heat of the moment should be broken. Is Carter Air truly your passion, or are you merely holding onto an old man's dream…and his bitterness?"

"How dare you say such a thing? His bitterness? You dumped him! In fact, you didn't even have the decency to tell him yourself at the time. He had to read your engagement notice in the local paper."

Alice felt a pang in her chest. "It was for the best."

"You'll have to forgive me if I disagree." Yasmin got up from the sofa and began to pace the floor, the layers of her gown swirling around her like a cloud. "Fine, I know I can't afford to break the contract. I'll go ahead with the wedding, but on one condition."

"And that is?"

"That our companies remain as two separate entities and Ilya and I never discuss business."

Alice rose and went to stand in front of Yasmin. "Your businesses are a big part of both your lives.

Not being able to share and discuss your day's work, your challenges and successes, means you'll only be sharing half a life together. Are you sure this is a wise decision?"

Yasmin's eyes darkened and her mouth firmed into a straight line before she spoke.

"It's the only way. If he won't agree to it then the wedding is off and you will release me from my contract with no penalty because while it would definitely harm my business if it was to be widely known I broke my contract with you, wouldn't the same be true for Match Made in Marriage? After all, Ilya is *your* grandson. In itself that would raise eyebrows if your involvement in this was made public, wouldn't it?"

Alice had to admire the girl's mettle. She inclined her head slightly. "And you'll accept my grandson's word that he will honor your request? I'm sure you've heard that his word is his bond."

Yasmin nodded.

"Fine. I will discuss it with my grandson."

"I have to say I'm surprised at how well you're coping," Valentin Horvath leaned over and whispered in Ilya's ear. "After all, it's not every day a man is rejected by his bride on first sight. Maybe I'm biased, being family and all, but I didn't think you were *that* ugly."

Ilya clenched his jaw and deliberately counted to ten before answering his cousin, who also happened to be one of his closest friends. Valentin headed up Horvath Pharmaceuticals in New York and was generally more serious in nature than his younger, more carefree brother, Galen.

"It's only to be expected that she would be nervous."

"And if she doesn't return?" asked Galen.

"She'll return."

"With Nagymama frog-marching her from behind, no doubt," Valentin said, using the family's Hungarian nickname for their grandmother.

Galen stifled a laugh. "Can't say I've seen Nagy move quite so quickly in the past few years."

"Protecting her investment, perhaps," his brother replied archly. "You know how personally she takes her matches."

Ilya rolled his eyes. Family ribbing was all very well and good—to be expected under the circumstances—but he was getting impatient. Where the hell was his bride?

He'd recognized Yasmin Carter the moment he'd turned around. So many thoughts had crossed his mind, the first being how stunningly beautiful she was in her wedding gown. Who knew that beneath the flight suits or jeans and a T-shirt he'd seen her wearing at the airfield, she could be so incredibly feminine, or so vulnerably fragile. That first glimpse of her today had appealed to an instinct his family constantly teased him about—his need to protect and provide for those he cared for. He hadn't expected to feel that for his bride immediately, but he had—deeply and viscerally. His response had made him want to follow her when she'd turned and left after her awkward pronouncement. It was only his grandmother's hurried whisper that she would deal with it that had prevented him from chasing Yasmin as she'd bolted from the room, even though every cell in his body had called on him to do so.

He looked at his watch again and fought not to start tapping his foot in impatience. The women had been gone twenty minutes now.

"The natives are getting restless," Valentin observed as he cast his eyes over the assembled family and friends who'd been able to make it on short notice. "It's a good thing you have the champagne flowing, Galen."

Galen was the head of Horvath's hotel and resort chain. He'd automatically switched into damage control mode the moment the wedding had gone off the rails. Ilya refused the offer of a waiter passing by with a tray of beverages. He needed a clear head today.

A movement in the doorway attracted his attention and he started toward his grandmother before anyone else noticed her.

"Is Yasmin all right?" he asked as his grandmother tugged him into the hallway.

"You recognized her?"

"Of course I did. While I'm left wondering what madness possessed you to match her to me, I've learned to trust you. But does she? She's more skittish than I would have thought."

"And so you ought to trust your grandmother. I only ever have your best interests at heart," Alice said, patting him fondly on the cheek. "We have a small problem."

A small problem? He would have thought his bride

running away from the ceremony was a bit more than that.

"She has a stipulation if the wedding is to proceed," his grandmother continued.

"And that is?"

"She's very protective of Carter Air. She will go ahead with this, provided that you two never discuss business together and that your companies remain two separate entities. Therefore, no mergers, no buyouts, no sharing of information."

"And that's it?"

In the grand scheme of things, it was nothing. Of course she'd want to protect her company. And though their families had bad blood between them, he wasn't interested in Carter Air as a takeover target and didn't wish Yasmin ill beyond the usual competition in the industry. It wasn't his style. He'd never understood why the cold war that had raged between his grandfather and Jim Carter, Yasmin's grandfather, had been carried on for generations. Ilya didn't believe in holding grudges. But even so he did wonder if his grandmother had some other ideas cooking beneath her halo of perfectly coifed silver hair.

"You agree, then?"

"Of course I agree, Nagy. Show me where to sign and I'll sign."

He saw relief in his grandmother's blue eyes. "Thank you, my boy. I think it's best if we keep this a verbal agreement for now, don't you? We don't want anything to muddy the waters should circumstances change, and thanks to your exemplary reputation,

Yasmin is prepared to accept your word. Now, go back inside and wait."

"We're going ahead?"

"We most certainly are."

Two

Yasmin fought the overwhelming sense of déjà vu that assailed her as she approached the double doors to the ballroom. This was it, her wedding day. She was actually going through with it. And now, hopefully, her problems would begin to fade away. Her business problems, at least. As for her personal ones, well, that was another story.

She hovered at the end of the carpet, sensed a movement at her side. Ilya.

"Yasmin Carter, will you marry me?" he asked, offering her his arm so he could accompany her down the aisle.

She looked up into his denim-blue eyes and saw only reassurance there. Strange that in business they were such fierce rivals, yet here he was offering her comfort, companionship. Marriage. It shouldn't have made sense—she barely knew the man—but in this moment he was the key that would hopefully unlock the door to her future.

"Yasmin?"

"Yes, I will marry you," she said in a voice she'd hoped would be firm and decisive, but that came out husky and with a faint tremor.

"Shall we?" He nodded toward the aisle.

She tucked her arm in his and together they walked slowly down the aisle toward the celebrant.

The ceremony itself passed in a blur. She supposed she said the right things at the right time, because before she knew it, Ilya was putting a blindingly brilliant wedding band on her finger and the celebrant was pronouncing them husband and wife.

Ilya leaned toward her. *Oh my, he's going to kiss me!* she thought, her heart kicking up to double speed in her chest. Unsure of what to do, she stood there, watching him come toward her with a twinkle in those intriguing eyes and an expression of humor mixed with determination on his face.

As he drew closer Yasmin felt his warmth and took in the scent of his cologne, the tang of pine with an underlying hint of sandalwood. And then his lips touched hers. Sensation rippled through her whole body and her breath caught in her throat. Time stopped. All that existed was the sensation of his kiss. And then, just like that, it was over. Too soon and yet not soon enough.

As he pulled away, there was a polite smattering

of applause together with whoops and hollers from Ilya's groomsmen. He might not be touching her right now, but every nerve in her body continued to party as if he still kissed her. It was madness and it was wonderful all at the same time. A roaring sound filled Yasmin's ears.

Her new husband leaned forward and whispered, "Breathe, Yasmin."

She took in one shuddering breath and then another before turning to accept congratulations from the few members of her staff—pretty much her only friends these days—who'd made it to the wedding. All the while she tried to come to terms with the avalanche of emotion that swept her along on its tumbling course. She was married. To Ilya Horvath. And the man was dangerous.

One kiss had scrambled her synapses. One. That's all it had taken. Was she so weak? So starved for male attention? Yasmin looked across at Ilya, her *husband*, and the tingle of desire he'd ignited in her dialed up a few notches. She felt a flush warm her cheeks as he turned from the person congratulating him and his gaze met hers. Yasmin swiftly averted her eyes.

Alice Horvath stood before her. Were those tears in the older woman's eyes? Surely not. Before Yasmin could say anything, Alice stepped closer.

"Congratulations, my dear, and welcome to the family. You're one of us now."

Alice pulled Yasmin into a firm hug, holding her close for several seconds before letting her go. Her words, however, settled into Yasmin's mind like a rock sinking in quicksand. Before she could reply, Ilya was back at her side.

"The photographer would like us to himself for a while. Nagy, will you excuse us?"

Yasmin wasn't sure how Ilya managed it, but within moments they were in the beautiful gardens overlooking the marina. She'd been excited when she'd learned that due to California's requirement that the couple apply for their license together, their wedding would instead take place in Washington State, where they could show up to apply separately, which satisfied the Match Made in Marriage condition of bride and groom first meeting at the altar. She'd always loved the area, with the trees, mountains and Puget Sound. The resort was as picturesque and breathtaking as she'd hoped, and the sounds of rigging clanking on the boats berthed in the marina peppered the sea-scented air.

"Are you okay?" Ilya asked. "You looked as if you could benefit from a breath of fresh air."

"I'm fine, thank you, but you're right. It's good to be away from the circus. I didn't know it would be so..."

"Overwhelming?" he said in a voice that sounded like he understood exactly how she was feeling.

She looked up at him. She was not a short woman, but in her flat-heeled slippers, he was a good head taller. "Yeah, overwhelming."

And she didn't just mean the ceremony. It was him—everything about him was more than she'd expected. Of course, she'd seen pictures of him. Even been in the same room with him a time or two when they'd attended aviation industry functions. But she'd never in a million years imagined being his wife. She dropped her gaze to his hands. He held a bottle of French champagne and a single glass. When had he grabbed those? she wondered as she noted his long fingers and how gracefully he poured the wine.

"Here," he said, handing the flute to her. "This might help."

Her skin was peppered with goosebumps—as if he'd touched her already, as if he'd traced those smooth fingertips across the swell of her breasts and lower, ever lower. Inside her corset she felt her nipples harden. A tiny gasp of surprise escaped her as a spear of longing arrowed straight to her core. Was this what Alice had meant when she said they belonged together? Did the woman have some kind of insight into the chemistry that attracted one person to another? The chemistry that made Yasmin feel as though she had about as much chance of avoiding her attraction to Ilya as an iron filing did a magnet?

She ripped her gaze from his hands and accepted the glass, lifting it straight to her lips and downing at least half the champagne in one gulp. The bubbles fizzed and danced along her tongue and down her throat, much as her blood danced more and more heatedly through her veins the longer she was around him.

This wasn't what she'd expected. This instant, engulfing need for a man she barely even knew, yet was now wedded to.

"Thirsty?" Ilya asked, cocking one brow.

A flush of embarrassment stained her cheeks, making her feel even more flustered.

"Something like that," she muttered and took another, more delicate, sip.

Before she could ask him why he didn't have a glass himself, the photographer and his assistant joined them. Yasmin took in as deep a breath as her corset would allow, grateful for the distraction.

The next hour passed in a blur of directions, unnatural poses and equally unnatural smiles. By the time the photographer called for one last pose, she'd drank far more of the bottle of champagne than anyone who'd skipped both breakfast and lunch out of nerves had a right to.

"Okay, people. How about a bit of passion?"

"He does know we only just met today, doesn't he?" Yasmin said to Ilya through gritted teeth. "We don't even know each other."

Ilya's arm slipped around her waist and he stepped in closer. "I think we can produce a reasonable facsimile of the feeling, don't you?"

He lowered his face to hers, his lips hovering a hairsbreadth away from her mouth. She could see the silver striations that radiated from his pupils and the rim of dark blue around his irises. He really had the most beautiful eyes she'd ever seen. His hand was strong against her back. Supporting. Warm. The warmth seeped slowly into her skin. A shiver ran up her back in total contrast. He might essentially be a stranger to her, but he affected her on a level that intrigued and frightened her at the same time.

His breath was a mere whisper against her lips, his gaze intense as he looked into her eyes. Involuntarily she raised her hand to cup his cheek, her palms tingling as she felt the bristles of his neatly trimmed beard against her fingertips. Her lips parted on a sigh and her senses primed themselves for that moment when their lips would touch.

“Perfect!” the photographer exclaimed joyfully, breaking the spell. “Now let’s go back inside for some group shots and the cutting of the cake.”

Yasmin blinked and let her hand drop to her side. Her other hand still clutched her bouquet in a death grip. What had nearly happened there? She wasn’t sure if she was grateful for the photographer’s interference or maddened by it. She shivered again. Even though it was early fall, and the day had dawned sunny and mild, clouds were gathering in the sky and the temperature had dropped markedly.

“Here, you’re cold. Let me put this on you.”

Before she could protest that they’d be inside soon, Ilya had stripped off his jacket and was draping it over her shoulders. The heat of his body transferred from the silk lining to her skin, leaving her feeling overly sensitive. A few drops of rain fell on his white shirt, rendering it transparent where they hit. She caught a glimpse of a dark nipple behind the fine cotton, felt a clench of need so intense it made her stumble as she started to move forward.

Ever the gentleman, Ilya steadied her. The photographer’s assistant rushed toward them with a massive white umbrella that Ilya accepted and held over them both. He guided her toward the doors leading to the main reception room. As soon as they were inside, she pulled off his jacket and thrust it toward him.

"Thank you. I don't need this now."

"It's okay to accept a little help from time to time."

"Said the man who has never had to ask for help from anyone, ever."

She smiled to soften her words but her meaning hung in the air between them. He had been born into a life of privilege. Certainly the privilege had been created by the hard work of previous generations and, she knew well, of the current generation, too. But had he ever truly wanted for anything?

"Besides," she continued, "you'll need to look your formal best for the reception."

He said nothing but shrugged the jacket back on. The resort's wedding planner hovered at the inner doors to the reception room.

"Are the two of you all ready?" she asked with an encouraging smile.

"As ready as we'll ever be, right?" Ilya replied with a crooked smile in Yasmin's direction.

She nodded, desperately trying to ignore the ridiculous sensations that poured through her. Anyone would think she was a sex-starved crazy woman if they knew how easily he sent her senses into overdrive. *And aren't you?* a little voice teased from the back of her mind. Okay, sure, she hadn't had a date in, what? Two years? And as for sex, well, it had been even longer. That didn't mean she had to melt like an ice cube on hot tarmac in the middle of July with just one look from him. Besides, he didn't appear to be similarly afflicted, she realized with a burst of chagrin. From now on she'd keep her ridiculous reactions very firmly under control. It couldn't be that difficult, could it?

Ilya observed his new wife with amusement. She was working hard to hold herself completely aloof, and yet the endearingly pretty flush of pink on her cheeks and her chest suggested she was just as attracted to him as he was to her. It would prove to be an interesting marriage, he decided. But would it be one that endured? His grandmother seemed to think so. He had yet to hear her reasons as to why, but Ilya knew that he and Yasmin at least had flying in common. The fact that they flew in direct competition with each other was another matter entirely.

Her gray eyes darted from one group of people to the next as they circulated through the room after the announcement of their arrival. He'd felt her entire body go rigid as they'd been introduced as Mr. and Mrs. Horvath.

"I'm not taking your name," she whispered fiercely as they finally settled at the head table.

"I didn't expect you to," he said to defuse her irritation. But mischief prompted him to add, "Would you prefer I took yours?"

Surprise chased the exasperation from her face. "Seriously? You'd do that?"

"If it was important to you," he answered sincerely. "I want this marriage to work, Yasmin. I don't yet know your reasons for entering into it, or why we've specifically been matched together, but I'd like to think the experts got it right and that we can make an honest go of this. I want a future that includes a family with the kind of companion I can't wait to see, whether it's when I wake or just before we fall asleep at night."

He hesitated. Was that too much, too soon? Judging by the startled expression on her face, perhaps it was. He'd surprised himself with that declaration, too. Still, he was the kind of guy who said what he wanted. He didn't hold with beating around the bush, and it was true. He wanted a family of his own. A wife who would be his partner in all things.

The reception continued with speeches interspersed between courses of the meal. He noticed she barely touched her food. And only one person stood up to speak for Yasmin. A woman Ilya recognized from the airfield—Yasmin's office manager, he recalled—who sat in her colorful sari at a table with a handful of others from Carter Air. His wife had no family here, he realized in surprise. He knew the grandfather who'd raised her had died a few years ago, but why hadn't her parents come today? Was their absence a sign of something deeper missing in her life? Did her reason for marrying stem from a need to create a family of her own?

He knew part of his reason in approaching his grandmother for a bride came from his wish to continue the family tradition of handing control of the corporation over to an heir or heirs. But finding the right woman had eluded him. He'd been engaged once, in college, but that had ended disastrously.

Ever since his father's death when he was sixteen, and his mother's subsequent withdrawal from parental duties as she went on a new quest to find love, he'd missed that feeling of being a piece of a small, tight-knit family unit. Yes, he'd had his grandmother, his aunts and uncles and cousins, but it wasn't the same as what he'd lost and what he craved to be a part of again.

He looked at Yasmin and felt a pull of sympathy. Her family life hadn't been much better. Ilya had met her irascible grandfather once and was surprised that Jim Carter and Eduard Horvath had been such great friends many years ago. They couldn't have been more different, from what Ilya could tell. His late grandfather had been a charismatic and driven man who always had an eye to the future and to expansion. He had lived, laughed and loved hard. On the flip side, Jim Carter had been quieter, withdrawn even, and his reluctance to embrace change had set Carter Air back in many ways. While his work ethic had never been in question, he'd lacked the vision and the willingness to expand and adapt to new horizons the way Eduard had. Their very differences had been what had made them such a great team until they'd fallen out over his grandmother and become enemies.

Yasmin, it seemed, had her own way of doing things with a liberal dose of her late grandfather's caution sprinkled in. Ilya knew one thing for certain—she was a damn fine pilot. He'd seen her in her vintage Ryan PT-22 Recruit at airshows and she'd taken his breath away. The Ryan had a reputation as an unforgiving aircraft but she handled hers as if it was a simply an extension of herself. Which made her an intriguing package, indeed, and begged the question: How many more layers would he uncover as he got to know his unconventional bride?

Three

Ilya leaned over and murmured in Yasmin's ear, "Everyone seems to be enjoying themselves."

Yasmin nodded, trying to ignore the frisson of awareness that tracked down the side of her neck as he spoke.

"Everyone except you," he added dryly.

"I'm fine," Yasmin insisted even as she clenched a fist in her lap.

She might be fine, but she hated being the center of attention like this. As if she was on display for approval by every member of his family. His cousins seemed nice enough, but she sensed a lot of confusion and perhaps even some veiled hostility from some of their parents' generation. And then there were the questions—like, where were her parents? Didn't they approve of her marriage?

Truth be told, she hadn't even been able to get hold of them to let them know about the wedding. They were somewhere in the wilds of South America the last she'd heard—chasing whatever dream they'd come up with this time. A traditional life filled with predictable choices was definitely not for them. Who knew? Maybe they would have approved of her adventurous approach to marriage, although she doubted it. Her father had tried to fit in to the mold her grandfather had cast for him but the two men had never been close, and in the end her father had left Carter Air, following his dreams with the woman he fell in love with and only returning long enough to leave his daughter in his father's care so she'd have stability and regular schooling.

She was grateful to her parents that they'd done that for her, even if her granddad had not always been the easiest man to live with. The transient life was definitely not her thing. She was more like the old man than she liked to admit—needing order, consistency, control. All of which had made today very hard to handle.

Ilya interrupted her thoughts. "Let's get out of here."

She turned to face her husband. "Can we do that?"

"I don't see why not. It's our wedding day. We can do whatever the hell we want, can't we?"

He held out a hand and she took it. His fingers closed around hers and he gently tugged her to her feet. Was this when their marriage would truly begin? In the honeymoon suite upstairs overlooking the marina and Puget Sound? Her stomach tightened into a knot of anxiety. As powerful as her attraction to him was, she knew she wasn't ready for this. Wasn't ready for *him*.

They managed to slip through one of the French doors to the patio outside. The earlier rain had passed, leaving the evening air damp and cold, heavy with the scent of woodsmoke. Ilya hastened to drape his jacket around Yasmin's shoulders again. She was grateful for the warmth as she followed him across the patio to another door that led to the hotel's main foyer.

"You know your way around," she observed. "It was all I could do today to negotiate my way from my room to the wedding."

He flashed her a smile. "You probably had other things on your mind."

Yasmin tried to ignore the way his smile made the corners of his eyes crinkle. It made him look even more impossibly handsome and made her wonder anew just how they were going to approach this first night together. She doubted she would have been as nervous had her husband been anyone other than the man standing before her now.

She squared her shoulders and took a deep breath.

"Let's go do this, then," she said with all the enthusiasm of an unrestrained wing walker heading into a double barrel roll.

Ilya laughed. "You don't need to sound quite so keen," he commented, as they headed to the elevators.

"I'm sorry," she said, blushing furiously. "I've never done this before. I'm not quite sure what the protocol is."

"It's okay," he assured her, his voice deep and even. "It's been a difficult day. Certainly not what I expected."

"What did you expect?" she asked as they stepped into the elevator.

"Not you, that's for sure. Not that I'm complaining," he added hastily.

"Well, I wasn't expecting you, either, if that's any consolation."

"Yeah, I think that was pretty obvious by your reaction," he teased.

Yasmin felt her lips tweak into a smile. It was the first genuine moment of humor she'd appreciated all day.

"You have a beautiful smile," Ilya commented as the doors swished open and they stepped out on her floor.

Their floor, she reminded herself. And just like that, the butterflies were back in her stomach and commencing an aerobatic maneuver. She suddenly wished there had been some kind of handbook issued explaining what happened next. Her smile died as the little voice in the back of her head told her she was an idiot. It was their wedding night. What did she think would happen next?

They reached the door to the honeymoon suite and Ilya produced a keycard from his pocket.

"My cases were brought up here during the reception," he said as they walked inside the beautifully appointed room. "I told them not to unpack."

"Not to unpack?" Yasmin repeated. "Aren't we supposed to be honeymooning here?"

"Did you particularly want to? I'm happy to stay if that's what you prefer but we have other options. We could disappear to Hawaii or even hide out at my home overlooking Ojai. The choice is yours."

Yasmin considered his words carefully. As much as she loved Washington, she felt like a fish out of water here with Ilya. Perhaps if she was back in California, in more familiar surroundings, this unusual marriage of theirs might begin to feel more usual.

She looked around the sumptuous suite where she'd felt like an outsider from the moment she'd arrived. She wasn't used to this world of wealth and glamour.

"No," she answered simply. "I don't want to stay here."

"So which is it to be? Hawaii or back to my place?"

He made it sound so simple. But then again, in his world, maybe it was.

"Let me change and pack."

"Do you need help?"

She was on the verge of refusing when she remembered the dress's multitude of hooks and eyes that Riya had helped her with.

"Thank you," she answered, turning her back to him. "Perhaps if you could undo the hooks for me?"

She heard his indrawn breath before he answered. "Sure. They look tricky. Let's see what I can do."

Yasmin braced herself for his touch. And there it was. He tucked his fingers into the top of her bodice and deftly worked the hooks and eyes apart. His hands were warm—didn't the man ever feel cold? She held the front of her dress against her.

"You're wearing a corset," he said as the back of her dress parted to reveal her undergarments. "Can you manage that on your own?"

Yasmin closed her eyes a moment. Having him undress her was proving to be sheer torture. "Perhaps if you can just undo the first few inches? I can manage the rest."

Ilya didn't answer. Instead, she felt his hands at her back again as he slowly worked his way through the fastenings. Yasmin dragged in a deep breath as the corset loosened and took a step forward.

"Thank you. I'll take it from here."

There was a tightness to her voice she couldn't hide and her heart hammered in her chest like a trapped bird. Curiosity pricked at the back of her mind; she wondered what it would be like if she turned around to face him. If she let her hands drop from where they held her bodice and just waited to see what would happen next. Fire raced along her veins again, licking tiny flames of need into aching life.

"Take your time," Ilya said. "I'll be waiting for you right here."

She felt him step away from her, heard the sound of leather creaking as he settled into one of the easy chairs. Yasmin forced herself to walk steadily to the bedroom. Once inside she closed the door behind her and released the breath she hadn't realized she was holding. She shook with reaction, fine tremors rippling through her body. If he hadn't withdrawn from her, she would have done it—she would have turned around.

She'd never been that kind of girl. Never one who followed her impulses. All her life she'd been focused and hardworking. She knew the consequences of not completing things to her best ability—knew, also, the rewards that came with achievement. So what had come over her that she was prepared to put all that aside and virtually throw herself at the stranger who waited on the other side of the door? The stranger who was her husband, she reminded herself. Did that make it right? She doubted it.

Yasmin let the gown fall to the carpet in a whoosh of expensive fabric, the hand-sewn crystals on her bodice winking at her reproachfully as she stepped out of the gown and toward the bed. Her hands worked feverishly on the final hooks securing her corset as she kicked off her slippers. When she was finally free of the garment, she let it drop to the floor, too. She rushed into the bathroom and turned on the shower, then shimmied out of her stockings and lace underpants.

Warm water coursed over her, flattening her short-cropped hair to her skull and washing her body free of the tension that gripped her. She wasn't that blushing bride who'd so intently embarked on this morning's adventure. That person had been a dreamer, not the doer Yasmin had always prided herself on being.

And the man waiting for her outside the bedroom? He was beautiful and appealing and all of the things that made her body react with unseemly eagerness. But he was also the enemy, and she'd do well to remember that.

Ilya began the final approach, relieved to see the helipad next to his house in the hills overlooking the Ojai Valley coming up ahead in the darkness. Yasmin sat next to him in the cockpit—silent, watching, stifling a yawn every now and then. He knew how she felt. The day had been exhausting, but they were nearly home.

They'd barely spoken since leaving the hotel. She'd taken longer than he expected to pack, and the woman who'd eventually emerged from the bedroom, dressed in long, dark pants, a cream linen blouse and battered leather flying jacket and wearing no makeup, had been a far cry from the bride he'd begun to undress.

His hand clenched on the controls, his fingers tingling as he remembered what it had felt like to undress her—how soft her skin was, how enticing her scent as they'd stood so close. It had taken every ounce of his considerable control not to lower his mouth to the curve of her neck where it flared into the feminine line of her shoulder. But he hadn't wanted to frighten her. If this marriage of theirs was going to work, he'd take it as slowly as she needed. He had a feeling it would be more than worth it.

He wondered what had brought her to Match Made in Marriage and made a mental note to check with his grandmother. Or maybe he should ask his wife. From now on, in all things she should be his first port of call, shouldn't she? In all things but their businesses.

Following the directions of the staff member marshalling him from the ground, he landed the chopper on the helipad.

"Welcome home, Mr. and Mrs. Horvath," Pete Wood, head of his air crew, said as he came forward to open the chopper door on Yasmin's side. "Watch your head, Mrs. Horvath."

"Call me Yasmin, please," Ilya heard his wife say tightly as she unlatched her harness, took off her headset and stepped down from the chopper.

He fought back a small smile. It gave him a surprising sense of pride to hear her called Mrs. Horvath. His wife. It sent a pulse of something powerful through him. As though he was a part of something new and exciting and uncharted. And in many ways, he was. He'd never been married before—hadn't even lived with a woman—which made the rest of his life with Yasmin pan out ahead of him as very much the great unknown.

How hard could it be? he reassured himself as he completed his shutdown procedures and then removed their suitcases from the rear of the chopper.

"Thanks for coming to marshal us in, Pete."

"No problem, sir. Congratulations on your marriage, both of you," Pete said with a beaming smile in Yasmin's direction.

She ducked her head shyly and a slight smile curved her lips. Ilya had noted that reticence around his family, too, and wondered if it had been just them. It looked as though she was like that with everyone—everyone connected with him, at least.

"Can I take your bags for you, Mr. Horvath?"

"No, it's okay, Pete. You head on home now."

Pete tipped his cap to Ilya. "Call me if you need me."

Ilya gave him a smile. "I'm officially on honeymoon. Hopefully I won't need to call you again until I'm back at work in two weeks' time."

"Sure thing, boss. Happy honeymooning."

Ilya walked over to Yasmin, who stood on the outer perimeter of the helipad. Behind him he heard Pete start the helicopter back up.

"If you don't want to be blown about, we'd better start walking toward the house. We'll take that path there," he suggested, nodding toward a path off to one side lined with garden lights.

"Are we stranded here?" Yasmin said, her eyes not straying from the helicopter.

"Does that bother you?"

"Should it?"

Ilya laughed. "No, it shouldn't, and no, we're not stranded." He gestured to the multicar garage off to the side of the house they were now approaching through the garden. "You can take your pick of vehicles in there should you feel the need to flee."

"Flee?" She arched a finely shaped brow as she looked at him. "What makes you think I'd want to?"

"Oh, perhaps the way you're twisting the strap of your bag."

She looked down at her hands. "I'm just nervous. Like I said before, I've never done this."

"Nor have I," Ilya assured her swiftly. "So let's agree to remain open with each other about how we're feeling, okay? Let me know, so I can relieve your nerves. Well, here we are."

Ilya approached the portico of his home. He'd fallen in love with the Mediterranean-style property nestled on forty acres of land the moment he'd seen it. It was a half-hour drive from the airport and Horvath Aviation—less time, of course, if he took a chopper—and now he'd get to share it with Yasmin. He set the suitcases down and pressed a finger on the reader at the front door before pushing the double doors open to reveal the entrance.

"Welcome to our home, Yasmin."

She started to move forward but he stopped her with a hand on her shoulder. "Allow me," he said and stepped closer to swing her up into his arms.

She stifled a squeak of surprise and hooked her arms around his neck as he crossed the threshold. She felt ridiculously light in his arms, but the press of her body against his had all the impact of a jumbo jet blast when it came to his senses. One hand curved around her ribcage, just beneath her breasts. Oh, yes, for all her slenderness she had curves, all right. What would she do if he followed tradition even further and kissed her again?

The brief peck on her lips after their ceremony had been both a tease and a torment for him. The second he'd felt her lips beneath his he knew he wanted to explore her further, but with a room full of family and friends looking on, he'd been forced to acknowledge there was a limit to what was acceptable in public. Even now that they were alone, her obvious apprehension about the day meant he would have to take things slowly, he reminded himself, as he set her back down on her feet again.

But then she shifted and leaned closer to him. His arms closed around her, pulling her against him, and he lowered his mouth to hers.

He felt a shock ricochet through him as her lips parted beneath his. She might be slight, but oh boy, did she pack a punch when it came to kissing. For a moment all Ilya could think of was the sweet taste of her, the softness of her lips, the texture of her tongue as it swept against his. He deepened the kiss, taking his time to relish the moment, to relish her. If this was a sign of things to come, they had a great deal to look forward to. She made his head swim with need, or maybe it was the blood heading to other parts of his body that made him so lightheaded.

He drew her lower lip between his teeth, sucking on it gently before tracing its fullness with his tongue. He wanted to do that all over her body. From her gorgeous, beautiful mouth to her breasts and lower. Just thinking about following his instincts left him aching with need—to pick her up again, take her upstairs to his bedroom and show her exactly how good their marriage could be.

But he felt her hesitation, that infinitesimal withdrawal. With the greatest reluctance he pressed one final kiss against her lips then let her go, steadying her on her feet as he did so. Yasmin's eyes were bright and her cheeks flushed.

Ilya walked to the entrance and picked up their suitcases, bringing them inside and closing the large wooden front doors behind him.

"Do you want the full tour now?" he asked. "Or would you rather wait until the morning?"

He watched her as she looked around the entrance and past it to the formal dining area and living room before turning back to face him again.

"I didn't expect your place to be so big," she said. "All this for just one person?"

"Well, when I bought it a couple of years ago I kind of had a vision of filling it with a family." He still had that vision and it grew sharper and clearer with every moment he spent in her company, even if it might be too soon to be thinking along those lines just yet. "How about you? Have you always wanted kids?"

"Yes," she answered emphatically. "Like you, I grew up an only child, but I didn't have cousins to fulfill a pseudo-sibling role as I understand yours did. I always swore that if I ever had children I would have more than one. I guess that's one of the reasons we were paired."

He breathed an inward sigh of relief. Some of his relationships had failed in the past because the women weren't at all interested in starting a family. It was vitally important to him that Yasmin be on the same page.

"So, the house—do you want to see more now? Maybe pick out a nursery?" he teased.

"It's probably a little too early for that," Yasmin answered with a chuckle. She stifled another yawn. "I'm sorry. Perhaps we can wait on the tour until morning."

"Sounds good. I'll show you your room. Follow me."

He led her up the stairs and a short way along a landing. He stopped outside the door to a guest bedroom and opened it. He gestured for her to precede him in and set her suitcase down on the blanket box at the foot of the large sleigh bed.

"You should be comfortable here. There's an en suite bathroom and my housekeeper will have stocked everything you need in terms of toiletries."

"We're…um…we're not sharing a room?"

"Not yet. Unless you'd like to?"

"I…" Yasmin's voice trailed off again.

"It's okay. I think you'd probably prefer that we get to know each other a little better before we take that step."

The words tripped glibly off his tongue, but inside his body protested strongly. He'd like nothing better than to whisk her down the hall to the master suite, lay her gently on his massive bed and show her exactly how well he wanted to get to know her. But the relief that spread across her face was about as effective as a cold shower.

"Thank you, I appreciate it."

"That doesn't mean I can't wish you a good-night, though. Sweet dreams."

Before she could say another word, he bent to kiss her gently, sweetly on her lips. He felt her lean toward him, but this time, rather than lose himself in the caress, he forced himself to keep it brief—to pull away and to leave them both wanting more. If he had to go to bed in a state of torment, then so could she. It was only fair.

He hesitated in her doorway on his way out. “My room is just down the hall if you change your mind.”

And with that parting comment he left her alone.

Four

It took Yasmin longer to get to sleep than she'd expected, considering how exhausted she'd been when Ilya had left her. But weariness aside, his kisses had fired up her imagination and as she lay between the cool crisp sheets of her lonely bed she couldn't help wondering what her wedding night could have been like if she'd just been brave enough to reach for him after that sweet goodnight and beg him to show her more.

She had no doubt he would be a consummate lover. From what she could tell, the man was incredibly accomplished in all that he did. And now she was married to him. She had the rest of her life to discover just how skilled he was. If they went the distance.

The next morning she rose and went downstairs, following the sound of a blender to a large kitchen.

Ilya stood at the granite kitchen counter, oblivious to her entry. She took a moment to watch him—to appreciate the way his Henley hugged the muscles of his shoulders and skimmed his pecs. A decrepit pair of jeans hugged his hips and she felt that all too familiar tingle through her body as she noticed how the denim had faded in certain areas. The blender stopped and Ilya looked up, a smile creasing his face as he saw her hovering in the doorway.

"Good morning," he said. "I hope you slept well."

"Thank you. I did, eventually."

Yasmin perched on one of the bar stools that lined the counter and watched as he poured two smoothies into tall glasses. Ilya pushed one toward her.

"I figured if we were so perfectly matched, you'd probably like one of these for breakfast," he said with a crooked grin. "But if you'd prefer bacon and eggs, I can do that, too."

"No, this is fine. I don't usually have breakfast anyway."

"Well, you'll need the energy for what I've got planned this morning."

"Oh?" She looked up at him, raising one brow.

"I love the way you do that," he said, reaching out and stroking her brow with a fingertip.

The sensation of his skin against hers made her hand tremble and she set her glass down on the counter with a sharp click. Ilya laughed and turned his attention to his smoothie, downing most of it in one gulp.

"And what is it you have planned for the morning?" Yasmin asked, picking up her glass again and taking a sip. “Oh, that’s good,” she exclaimed in surprise. “What did you put in it?”

“First question first. We’re going for a hike. Have you got hiking boots or something suitable in your suitcase? If not, we can do something else. As to the smoothie, that’s a closely guarded secret,” he said with a sly wink. “One day I might let you in on it.”

She chuckled. “Well, in the meantime I shall just appreciate your culinary expertise. And, as to shoes, I have something suitable for a hike. What time do you want to head out?”

“Probably in half an hour or so. Think you can be ready by then?”

“I was born ready,” she answered, finishing off her smoothie and hopping down from her seat.

“Good to know,” Ilya responded.

His voice was deep and reverberated through her in a way that sent her senses scrambling. She had the distinct feeling they were speaking along completely different lines. Yasmin took her glass over to the sink and rinsed it out. It was easier to fake being busy with something than it was to acknowledge exactly what kind of an effect her new husband had on her.

“This is a nice kitchen,” she said, striving for more neutral conversational territory. “Did you have it installed or did it come like this when you bought the house?”

“I bought the house pretty much as you see it,” he said. “With the exception of the furnishings and art. Why don’t I show you the rest before we head out?”

She nodded and followed him as he led the way

out of the kitchen and through to a casual sitting area. A massive television dominated most of one wall.

"Wow," she exclaimed. "All you need is a cooler in the side of your chair and you'll be living every man's dream, won't you?"

"Hey, when I watch the air races I want to feel like I'm in them, not just a spectator."

"I understand. Although nothing quite beats the real thing."

"Speaking of which, are you going to take me up in your Ryan anytime soon?"

"I heard you don't like being a passenger—that you prefer to hold on to the controls yourself."

She said the words lightly, but she understood them on her own level. She'd spent years side by side with her grandfather restoring the Ryan to flying condition and had worked really hard to earn her rating to fly it. No one took that plane up but her.

"Where did you hear that?" Ilya asked, his brows drawing into a straight line.

"Oh, it's pretty common knowledge around the airport. You know how people talk."

"What else do they say about me?" Ilya asked, moving closer to her.

She could feel the heat that emanated from his body. It was like a magnet, drawing her closer. She nearly always felt cold, but with him around, she doubted she'd ever need an extra layer again.

"Oh, that you're a hard worker and a reasonable boss."

"That's it?"

"Hey, you wouldn't tell me what was in the smoothie,

so I'm not sharing all my secrets. A girl's got to hold something back, right?"

He laughed again and Yasmin felt her lips kick up in an answering smile.

"So I'm an overbearing pilot, a hard worker and a *reasonable* boss."

Her grin widened at the chagrin with which he said the word *reasonable.* "I never said overbearing. But if the shoe fits…?"

He reached out to catch her shoulders with his hands. Heat seared through her top and penetrated her skin. Her heart rate kicked up a notch. Was he going to kiss her again? Part of her hoped he would, while the other… The other part wasn't ready to face the tumult of sensation he set off in her. It was a weakness she needed to learn to shore up, and swiftly, if they were to remain on an even playing field when it came to this marriage. She had too much to lose otherwise.

To a lot of people, marrying sight unseen just to save her business was an extreme measure. Heck, even to her it was extreme. But to win the Hardacre contract, she had to be married. It was as simple as that. It was frustrating that, in this day and age, her business was held hostage by Wallace Hardacre's wandering eye and his wife's jealousy. But if getting married meant she'd win the five-year exclusive contract ensuring her company had the income stream to not only keep it afloat but eventually allow it to expand and create more jobs, she was prepared to do it.

All she'd had to do then was find a husband. Fast. She'd just never expected that husband to be Ilya Horvath.

Ilya snapped his fingers, dragging her out of her reverie.

"Earth to Yasmin. I feel like I lost you there for a moment."

She forced a smile. "Sorry, just thinking about my grandfather," she fibbed.

"I never met him but I heard he was a wizard mechanic. Not an aircraft engine he couldn't fix, right?"

She nodded. "Yeah. He was always better at mechanics than people."

"Was it hard growing up with him?"

"Yes and no. Obviously I missed my mom and dad. They'd cruise by when they were in the area, still do occasionally. But Granddad gave me stability, which I didn't have with them. And he taught me the value of silence."

"Is that a hint?"

"Oh, heavens, no. Not at all. It's just some people seem to need to fill a silence with noise, rather than simply letting the silence fill them for a change."

Ilya nodded. "I think I know a few people like that. Come on, let me show you the rest of the place, then we can head out in the hills."

She was fit and strong, Ilya thought appreciatively as they reached the crest of the hill that would afford them the best view across the valley. And she didn't complain, either.

"That was quite a climb," Yasmin said, as she stopped and put her hands on her hips.

Her breathing was only slightly labored and she'd

barely broken a sweat even though the temperatures had begun to climb into the seventies very soon after they'd started hiking.

"It's worth it for the view," Ilya commented as he came to stand beside her.

And he wasn't just talking about the stunning Ojai Valley vistas, either. The woman standing next to him was a picture of perfection. She glowed with natural good health and vitality, a far cry from the kinds of women who moved in his circles. At the back of his mind he couldn't help but feel there was something familiar about her, too. But of course there had to be, he told himself as he turned his gaze from her to the valley that spread before them. They worked at the same airport. They'd both been fed stories of how their families had been friends then feuding rivals. They knew of each other, even if they didn't actually know each other. Even so, the little niggle persisted that he knew her from somewhere else.

"You were so lucky last year's fires missed your home," Yasmin said, looking around at the flora fighting to regenerate on the hills around them.

"I was luckier than a lot of people."

"Your property looks like an oasis from up here," she commented.

"It certainly feels like it after a hard day in the office."

He heard her breath hitch. "We agreed not to talk about work, remember?"

"Right. My mistake."

He clenched his jaw. It had only felt natural to mention work. After all, it had taken up more than half of every day of his adult life. It was going to be harder than he thought to compartmentalize things, to exclude her from what was essentially the core of his world. But then again, he reminded himself, in time she would become the core of his world—wouldn't she?

A tiny animal sound came from somewhere behind them.

"Did you hear that?" Yasmin asked, looking around.

"Yeah. There it is again."

Ilya walked cautiously toward the source of the noise, wary in case the animal was unfriendly. Yasmin showed no such care. She pushed past him into the undergrowth.

"Oh look, it's a puppy. The poor baby."

She scooped the mess of dirt and multicolored fur up into her arms and cradled it to her. The puppy whimpered.

"Is he hurt?" Ilya asked, stepping forward.

It maddened him that people could be so cruel as to abandon their animals, and this one looked very definitely abandoned. The puppy bore a narrow blue collar, which hinted that at some stage it had had an owner who cared enough to buy it one. There was a road that passed not too far from this point. It had probably been dumped along there. Possibly even thrown from a passing car if the grazes on his paw pads were anything to go by.

"Not too badly, I think. But he'll be thirsty, poor baby. I wonder how long he's been up here."

Ilya poured some of the water from his bottle into

the palm of his hand and offered it to the puppy. The animal weakly lapped it up. The little guy was probably dehydrated. Ilya kept adding a little trickle of water until the puppy stopped drinking.

"What are we going to do with him?" Yasmin asked, stroking the puppy's grubby head.

"I guess we'll take him to the vet to be checked out and maybe see if he was stolen before he was dumped. There might be someone missing him. If he was stolen we'll know more."

"And if he wasn't?"

She looked at him with such an expression of yearning in her eyes that it made him wish he could grant her every wish.

"Then we'll keep him."

"I've never had a dog," she admitted, pressing a kiss to the top of the puppy's head and earning a sloppy kiss in return. "But I've always wanted one."

"First, let's get him to the vet."

Ilya put out his hands to take the puppy from her. The animal really was a sad little bag of bones and hair. Ilya only hoped that it didn't have any underlying problems. He could see that Yasmin had already lost her heart to the little guy. He didn't want to see it broken if the puppy had to be euthanized. It didn't matter how much money it took, he decided. They'd be bringing this little one back home.

Five

When Yasmin and Ilya returned from the vet, they were both covered in grime from the puppy. They'd left him for a thorough checkup and to be rehydrated. The animal wasn't microchipped and didn't appear on any lost pet registers so it didn't look like he could be returned to his owners. Not that they deserved him if they had been the people who dumped him in the first place, Yasmin thought with a surge of anger.

She'd been pleasantly surprised by Ilya's reaction, though. She'd seen a side of him she hadn't known existed before today. Everything she'd ever heard about him in the past had pointed to his being an over-entitled, calculating person. Not someone who could show so much compassion to an abandoned animal. And certainly not someone she would ever have seen herself married to, let alone potentially happily married to. She didn't want to admit she could be wrong about him—after all, once she made up her mind, she didn't usually waver. But she needed to form her own opinions of the man she'd married, and so far he was shaping up to be very interesting, indeed.

"I don't know about you, but I feel like I could do with another shower," Ilya said, closing the front door behind him. "But before we do that, let's get you into the biometric security database so you can come and go as you please."

He invited her to the keypad and pressed a few buttons before asking her to put her finger on the sensor.

"There, that's all done."

"And in a power outage?"

"Battery backup."

"And if that fails?"

"Generator."

She pursed her lips. "Do you always think of everything?"

"Contingency plans are my thing."

"Is there a particular reason for that?"

"I don't like being caught unprepared. It happened once in my life and I swore to always be primed for whatever could happen next from then on."

"Sounds serious."

"It was."

Yasmin looked at Ilya—saw the shadows that passed through his eyes.

"Do you want to talk about it?" she prompted gently.

"Not really, but you deserve to hear it from me

rather than secondhand from anyone else. In fact, I'm surprised you don't already know."

"About what?"

"The day my father died." Ilya sighed and rubbed his fingers over his beard. "I was sixteen and he was giving me a flying lesson. He just died. Right there next to me. His head dropped forward, he stopped breathing and his heart stopped beating. Just like that. One minute we were talking, the next he was gone. I couldn't do a single damn thing to help him. Even if I'd known CPR, it wasn't like I could start it right there in the cockpit. I had to land as quickly as possible to give him a chance, so I radioed for help and they talked me down."

"Oh, no. That must have been terrifying for you."

"I'd done a couple of landings before, so while it wasn't the best of landings, we got down safely. But it was too late for my dad. They said he suffered catastrophic heart failure and there was nothing that I could have done."

Silence fell between them and Ilya shook his head.

"Anyway, that was nearly twenty years ago. It's well and truly in the past and it's part of the reason why I like to be prepared for any eventuality now."

"I'm really sorry about your dad, Ilya."

He looked at her, his intense blue eyes piercing her as if he could see through all her shields to the genuine compassion she felt for his loss.

"Thank you." He gave her a bittersweet smile. "You know, most people, when they hear what happened, focus on the flying and on how I got the plane down. Very few actually remember I lost my father that day."

Yasmin tried to ignore the tug in her chest. "Well, I don't think anyone could ever accuse me of being like most people."

"You're not at all like I expected."

"That makes us even, then," she answered as lightly as she could. Before he could reply, she started up the stairs. "I'm going for that shower you suggested."

She felt his eyes boring into her back, as if he was reassessing her in some way. It made her wonder exactly what he had expected when he realized she was to be his bride.

In her room, Yasmin gathered up some clean clothes and went into the bathroom. His housekeeper had been in already and changed the towels. The woman had to be a ghost because Yasmin hadn't met her yet, but she could certainly tell where she'd been. She put her things on the vanity and reached to turn on the shower. Her wedding ring caught the light and the diamonds sparkled brightly.

Unused to wearing jewelry, Yasmin was surprised at how quickly she'd become accustomed to the ring. It wasn't something she would have picked for herself but she certainly wasn't averse to wearing it. The design was very low profile, so it wouldn't catch on anything, and the baguette and round diamonds that crested the top of the platinum setting appealed to her hidden sense of whimsy.

She quickly disrobed and stepped into the shower, rinsing away the perspiration of the morning and the grime she'd picked up from the puppy. She wondered how he was doing. The poor thing had been so very listless but the vet, apparently another of Ilya's cousins, had been reassuring and said she expected him to make a full recovery in a few days' time.

Yasmin lathered up some soap and stroked it over her body, remembering just how gently Ilya had held the pup when he'd taken it from her on the walk back to the house. His hands fascinated her. Broad but with long tapered fingers, they contained such strength and capability. What would it feel like when he touched her intimately? she wondered.

Her pulse kicked up a beat and her insides tautened on a swell of desire. Only time would tell—if they lasted that long—she told herself as she switched the spray to a cooler setting and rinsed off quickly before drying and dressing herself again. There was still the incompatibility clause to contend with, although based on this morning's adventure, they seemed to be getting along okay.

But one morning did not a marriage make, she reminded herself firmly. She grabbed her cell phone from her bedside table and quickly checked her email, flicking through the congratulatory messages from her colleagues at Carter Air. There was one there from someone she didn't know. *Strange*, she thought as her finger hovered over the message, debating whether to open it or send it to spam. Curiosity got the better of her and she opened the unread message.

You had no right to marry him.

A sick feeling lodged in Yasmin's throat. Sheer instinct made her press Delete but then she went into the trash file to find out who had sent it. The sender's address was linked to a widely used email provider and there was nothing in the moniker attached to it, *hisgirl*, that rang any bells. Yasmin hit Delete again, removing the message from her email server completely. It was just some sicko with nothing better to do, she told herself as she returned downstairs and put the correspondence to the back of her mind.

She found Ilya out in the loggia by the pool. Grapevines, laden with bunches of plump fruit, grew over wooden rafters that sheltered the area. He rose from a chair as she approached.

"I just made a call to Danni. She tells me the puppy is on a drip with dextrose and he's already starting to look more alert."

"Oh, that's great news. Thanks for checking up on him."

"No problem. I thought you'd want to know. Danni said she'll give me an update this evening. By tomorrow she thinks he might be able to take a bit of food."

"And then can we have him?"

"That'll be up to her."

"Of course," Yasmin was quick to agree. "He's getting the best care possible, which is just as it should be."

"I'm surprised you never had a pet as a kid. You seem very invested in this one."

"Granddad wasn't keen on animals. Just another mouth to feed, he always said."

* * *

Ilya looked at her in surprise. Was that how old man Carter had thought about his granddaughter, too? When her parents had left her with him, had she just been another mouth to feed, or had he genuinely loved her?

"Speaking of feeding, Hannah has made us some lunch."

"Hannah? Is that your housekeeper?"

"Yes, she thought she'd remain scarce while we're still on honeymoon."

"She needn't stay away on my account."

Ilya laughed. "Sick of me already?"

"That's not what I meant," Yasmin protested.

"Just teasing you. You're going to have to get used to that."

"I'm not used to teasing, period. Anyway, I reiterate, she doesn't have to skulk around avoiding us."

"When you get to meet her, you'll know that Hannah never skulks," he said on a chuckle. "She just thought we'd benefit from time to get to know each other. She'll pop in every few days, freshen up our supplies and do a bit of housework."

"I can do housework. I don't expect to be waited on."

"Not even by your husband?"

To his surprise, Yasmin's cheeks grew flushed.

"Not by anyone," she said firmly.

"That's a shame, but you're going to have to get used to it because I've been appointed your waiter for this afternoon. Take a seat and I'll go get lunch."

"I can help."

He walked around behind her and put his hands on her shoulders, guided her to a chair facing the pool and gently pressed her into it.

"I've got this. Just relax."

Yasmin choked out a laugh. It had a slightly bitter ring to it. "I'm not used to relaxing. I'm more used to working."

"Everyone needs a break," he said lightly. He wasn't going to be the one to point out that she'd brought up work this time. He hated that they had to walk on eggshells around the topic. The longer he thought about it, the crazier it seemed. But then again, they were business rivals, which was going to make this a very interesting marriage all around.

He removed the lightly grilled salmon from the oven, divided it into two equal pieces and plated it. He set the plates on a large tray, then added a bowl of salad together with a small jug of lemon-caper sauce for the salmon before taking it all outside.

"That looks good," Yasmin commented with a great deal of interest as he approached.

"Trust me, Hannah is an incredible cook. I'd be half the man I am today without her," he answered with a smile. "How about you serve up our salad and I'll go get us drinks."

He went back to the kitchen and grabbed the ice bucket, together with two glasses and a particularly good German Riesling he'd been saving for a special occasion. Returning to the table he pulled the cork and poured two measures of wine. He gave one glass to Yasmin then held his up in a toast.

"To us," he said simply.

She hesitated a moment, her eyes not quite meeting his, but then she seemed to come to a decision and she clinked her glass against his. "Yes, to us."

For some reason her response made him relax. He hadn't even realized he'd been on tenterhooks until he'd waited those extra few seconds. He took a sip of the wine. It shouldn't matter so much already, but he wanted to be fully invested in this marriage. He had told his grandmother he was ready for it, ready to commit to one person for the rest of his life, and according to her she'd found him The One. He was the kind of guy who, once committed, gave it his everything. Was Yasmin ready for that? Ready for him? Maybe if he understood her reasons for entering into their match he could be sure they were completely on the same page, but until then he knew he'd be holding a piece of himself back.

He'd been hurt. He'd believed his ex-fiancée had loved him the same way he'd loved her. That she'd wanted the same things. But in the end it had turned out that she was a fake, and not only a fake but a cruel one into the bargain. He didn't want to make that same mistake again. It had made him wary of relationships, of trusting anyone outside of the tight-knit circle of his family.

Could he trust Yasmin?

Six

Yasmin continued to swim against the tide of the pressure jets in the pool. Her arms and shoulders were beginning to burn but she had to rid herself of the frustration and tension that had become her companion over these past few days.

There'd been another email since the one a few days ago. Again, she'd been tempted to delete it unread. Again, she'd opened it. The message had been succinct.

Leave him!

Yasmin had the strong feeling that *or else* was implied. She wondered who the heck *hisgirl* was. Clearly someone who thought they had a prior claim on Ilya.

Well, that someone could take a long walk off a short pier. Which made Yasmin realize she felt oddly proprietary about her husband of only a few days.

Yesterday, they'd visited the puppy at the vet's, and he was coming along quite literally in leaps and bounds. His stomach was taking a while to adjust to solid food again so Danni was taking an extra day or two just to ensure he was one hundred percent before releasing him. Ilya and Yasmin would initially foster him, then hopefully become his full-fledged owners if no one came forward to claim him soon.

Watching Ilya with the puppy really tugged at her heartstrings. This big man who had such a powerful reputation in the aviation world was an absolute pushover when it came to the puppy. It seemed as if Ilya wore a different face for each different situation he found himself in, which made her wonder about the face he showed her.

He'd been solicitous toward her, but since the night of their wedding he'd made no further move to touch her or kiss her again, and quite frankly, it was driving her crazy. Her nights had been peppered with dreams of the two of them, limbs entwined, lips fused in passion—and unfulfilled demands had woken her every morning, leaving her seething with frustrated need.

She'd had sex before. Quite liked it on occasion. But she'd never missed it when she hadn't been in a relationship with someone, partly because she could always throw herself into her work. And she'd certainly never suffered from this level of torment before. Nor had she ever found herself sizing someone up—in this case, her husband—and wondering about how the play of his muscles would feel beneath her fingertips or her tongue. Or wondering at the shape of his butt as he bent to remove some plate of deliciousness from the oven for their evening meal together.

Hence the swimming. Between that blasted email and her unrequited sexual needs she had to find release somewhere. She didn't want to spend all her time mooning over her husband's all-too-few masterful kisses or the shape of his body. Well, maybe she did, but it wasn't going to help her any, was it?

Her muscles screaming, she did a flip turn, slowly swam to the opposite end of the pool and hauled herself up onto the edge.

"I was beginning to think you'd developed fins and gills," Ilya said from above her.

She lifted her head and looked up. Her mouth dried instantly. He was wearing a pair of swim shorts that exposed his long, tanned legs, and above the waistband all she could see was an expanse of skin and muscle.

"Gotta get my exercise somehow," she muttered, accepting a towel from him and averting her gaze as she dried off.

"Our daily hikes not enough for you? Maybe I need to set a more challenging pace," he teased.

He sat down beside her on the edge of the pool and dangled his legs in the water. Her skin was cool from being in the water for so long and she could feel the heat coming off him in waves. How was it that he was literally so hot? It was like his internal thermostat was constantly set on high. Her one-piece suit clung to her body like a second skin and she felt her nipples tighten against the wet fabric.

"It's okay," she said. "I enjoy the walks."

"Me, too. You're good company."

"Just as well, huh? It would make life difficult if we didn't get along."

Ilya propped himself up on his arms and turned his face to the sun. With the light streaming over his body, he looked like a gilded warrior god of ancient times. Yasmin felt that all-too-familiar tug through her body, that clench deep in her core.

"I've been meaning to ask you something," he started and straightened to look her in the eye.

Yasmin felt a frisson of wariness. "And that is?"

"Why did you apply to Match Made in Marriage? After all, you're a good-looking woman who runs her own business. I haven't seen any evidence of unusual traits or habits that would be majorly off-putting to anyone."

"Majorly? Oh, so you think I have some minor off-putting traits?" she asked on a laugh.

"You know what I mean. Getting to know you is interesting. Like, I never realized you were such a nerd at school."

"I never told you I was a nerd."

"No, but this morning while we were on the trails you did tell me about winning the science prize and the math expo and—"

"Okay, so I was a nerd."

"And you're very good at dodging a direct question."

She was about to protest when she realized that was exactly what she had done. She looked down to the end of the pool.

"I should turn the jets off."

"And there you go again. It's okay. They can stay on for now."

"Fine. In answer to your first question, I went to Match Made in Marriage because I didn't trust myself to find the right guy for me."

That was partially true, at least. Her own track record with men was not the best. It didn't help that she'd never really considered what she wanted out of a relationship. That, combined with her reluctance to allow people to get close to her and really share her life, tended to send her beaus away in frustration. People didn't like being shut out all the time. And she'd thought Match Made in Marriage would be safe, especially with its out clause if they turned out to be incompatible. Of course, if she'd known Alice Horvath was behind the matches she probably wouldn't have approached them at all.

"How about you?" she asked.

"I guess my reason was similar. I trusted Nagy to find the right woman for me."

"I heard you guys call her that. What is it? Russian?"

"No, Hungarian. My great-grandfather was a scientist and lecturer. Prior to the outbreak of World War II he began to grow uneasy about what was happening across Europe. He decided to move his family out of Hungary and to the States. Even though she was mostly raised here in California, my grandmother still clings very much to the old ways. More so as she grows older, I guess."

He fell silent for a bit then spoke again. "Do you think Nagy got it right, pairing us?"

"It's early days, but we're not an abject failure yet, are we?"

"No. So, why now? What made you decide this was the time you wanted to get married?"

Boy, he was like a dog with a bone on the subject, wasn't he? Yasmin raked her mind for a suitable response. There was no way she'd tell him that she had to marry now because of the Hardacre contract. Had Horvath Aviation pitched for the same business? How would Ilya feel when she won it out from under him? she wondered. Especially if he knew he'd handed it to her on a platter by marrying her. *You haven't got the contract yet*, she reminded herself.

In answer to his question, she shrugged. "What can I say? I'm thirty-two years old. Yes, I know that's still young but, like most people, I want a family and stability. Now felt like the right time."

She paused before she inadvertently let too much out. Her current stability hinged on the Hardacre contract but she couldn't let Ilya get a whiff of that information. She let out a breath before continuing, knowing she'd have to dig deep into a part of her she kept hidden, even from herself, if she was to satisfy Ilya's curiosity.

"I didn't have the most traditional of upbringings. I knew I had someone who loved me, even if Granddad wasn't the best at showing it. But I have to admit to having had some envy for the other kids at school. The ones whose parents came to sports days or helped in class. Some of the kids used to complain about it, that their parents were always right there. They had no idea how lucky they were. It just seemed so *normal*, y'know?"

"And being brought up by your grandfather made you different among your peers, didn't it? That and the fact you were such a nerd." He smiled and leaned over to bump shoulders with her, taking any imagined sting out of his words. "I get it. I never thought about things that way. I mean, my parents didn't show up at everything but they put in an appearance when it mattered enough to me to ask them to. Until my dad died, anyway."

Yasmin drew her knees up to her chest and wrapped her arms around them. "Granddad was always sparing with his approval, but it didn't stop me working hard to earn it. In its own way, that set me up for life. You can't always expect sunshine and lollipops, right? You need to learn to roll with disappointment and get up and just keep going."

Ilya listened to Yasmin and felt a pang of sympathy for the child she must have been growing up. He knew Jim Carter had been a cantankerous old bastard, but not to show encouragement to a little girl trying to find her place in his life? That was downright mean. Ilya's children would never doubt that he was behind them in whatever they chose to do. And, yes, while it was his dream that they would follow him into Horvath Aviation, as he had done with his father and he with his father before him, Ilya certainly wouldn't force them to do it. Encourage them, maybe, but force them? No.

"What about you, Ilya? What made you use your grandmother's service? I could use the same argument you did. It's not as if you're all that ugly or anything."

He could recognize deflection along with the best of them. Yasmin was obviously uncomfortable being the topic of discussion. If he was going to earn her trust and get down to the layers that really made up the woman, he was going to have to give a little of himself, too. He swallowed. Opening up to someone who was essentially a stranger, even though the license said they were married, didn't come easily. Growing up a Horvath had taught him to be careful around people, especially those who thought he was an easy meal ticket because of his family's wealth. The one time he'd let his guard down… No, he didn't want to waste this beautiful day thinking about past mistakes.

"Thanks for the compliment," he responded lightly. "I guess my reasons are the same as yours. I'm thirty-five. Again, not old, but I'm ready for the next stage of my life. I'm ready to be part of a partnership and all that brings—including children. Family is really important to me." He barked a humorless laugh. "*Everything* to me, to be completely honest with you. I just want the chance to do it right the first time. And people can be so fake. The lines are so blurred now it's hard to tell who's being real and who isn't."

Yasmin's face was set in serious lines and she looked as if she was about to say something, but she was distracted by a notification tone from her cell phone sitting on a nearby chair.

"Will you excuse me? I'm expecting this."

"Sure."

Ilya slid forward on the pool edge and allowed himself to slip into the water. It was a bit of a comedown—having bared a piece of his soul only to be interrupted by an incoming message on her phone. But, he reminded himself, it was early days yet.

He sank down in the water, letting the silky softness of it close over his head and caress his skin before he popped back up to the surface. He slicked his hair back off his forehead and looked across at Yasmin, who was standing by the chair. Nope, the water definitely wasn't cold enough, he thought as he let his gaze roam from her bare feet and up her long, slender legs. Even though she wore a modest one-piece suit, there was no mistaking the lean muscles of her body. The woman looked after herself, there was no denying it.

His gaze traveled over the gentle swell of her hips, to her narrow waist and then upward to where her swimsuit cupped her breasts. His mouth went dry and he dunked himself again, feeling just a little disgusted with himself for staring at her like some horny schoolboy. This time when he surfaced he realized she was still standing in the same position but something wasn't right. Yasmin had her phone in hand and was staring at the screen with a stricken expression on her face.

"Everything okay?" he asked, pulling himself up onto the edge of the pool and getting up to check on her.

Yasmin put her phone face down on the table and looked up at him, swiftly composing her features.

"Why shouldn't it be?"

He noticed she didn't answer his question. "You looked upset. Is there anything I can do?"

"You can do?" she repeated before shaking her head. "No, it's nothing. Really."

"It didn't look like nothing. If you want to talk—"

"Really," she emphasized. "There's nothing wrong. Go, have your swim. I think I'll go upstairs and get changed."

He watched her grab her phone and retreat—there was no other word for the way she left the pool area. There had been something on her phone that had bothered her, he knew it as surely as he knew the maximum fuel uptake of every aircraft in his fleet. And, like the man who knew his business inside and out, he wanted to know Yasmin inside and out, too.

Eventually he'd find a way to break through the barriers she had around her. It wouldn't be easy, but something told him that if he persevered, it would be worth it. But first he needed to earn her trust. And that might be the hardest thing of all.

Seven

Yasmin couldn't get to her room fast enough. The moment she was upstairs she secured her door and opened the email. And there it was. There were no words, no subject header. Just that photo.

A shudder ran through her body from the top of her head to the soles of her feet. She'd believed that dreadful night was behind her. That no one had any further cause to hark back to what she'd done. Oh, sure, she had behaved under extreme pressure. And her desperation to be included in the sorority made up of all the cool girls had been the catalyst for what would lead to her greatest shame.

Why would anyone hold on to something like this? And why bring it up now? She'd changed universities; she'd moved back West; she'd severed all ties. In fact, the very thought of coming face-to-face with anyone who had been there that night, egging her on to drink another shot every time she got a question wrong in that stupid quiz they made her and the other pledges take, was unfathomable.

Bile rose in Yasmin's throat as she looked at the photo. She looked just like any other college girl having a good time, but even though she'd already been feeling the effects of the vodka shots, she'd been horribly uncomfortable posing with the sex toy someone had thrust in her face that night. But her desire to win at any cost had seen her outlast her fellow pledges and the challenges had just kept on coming. She'd fulfilled that challenge, and the next one, and the one after that, but by the time they'd made her enter the lake and swim out to the pontoon, blindfolded, she'd also been highly intoxicated. The alcohol in her system, the cold of the water and her sense of disorientation at being blindfolded had combined in a perfect storm that had led to her losing consciousness before she could complete the challenge.

She had no idea who'd rescued her from the water, or who had called the ambulance that had taken her to the hospital where her stomach had been pumped and she'd been rehydrated and treated for hypothermia. She did remember the letter she'd received from the sorority, though. The one saying that, on reflection, they felt she wasn't the caliber of student they were looking to have join them.

It had been hard, going back to class and facing the pitying looks from some of her peers. Worse was the outright laughter from others. These people had seen her at her worst, at her most desperate, her most vulnerable—and she knew she couldn't continue at college in that environment. At the end of the semester she'd transferred back to California and completed her education closer to home. Her grandfather had never questioned her choices; he'd been only too pleased to have her close again. His health had begun to fail, and his reluctance to follow doctor's orders and make simple changes in his lifestyle aggravated existing conditions. And, as soon as she graduated, she'd gone to work with him full-time.

She'd honestly believed that what had happened out East was behind her, but now it appeared it wasn't. Even though it was more common now to report extreme hazing incidents for the cruel bullying they were, back then she'd been so ashamed of her own desperation to be one of the "in" crowd, and what she'd been prepared to do to be accepted, she'd never made a report to the campus authorities or the police. And now it was coming back to bite her.

It seemed obvious that her marriage to Ilya had triggered this, but who was behind the *hisgirl* email address? What did they hope to gain? Worse, what would happen if this photo, and potentially others—because she knew there'd been a lot of people taking pictures of her that night—were shown to anyone else? Anyone, for example, like her new husband, her employees—or the Hardacres? She'd lose all her hard-earned respect from everyone.

Yasmin hadn't responded to any of the emails she'd

been sent so far. She hadn't wanted to engage with whoever was behind this, but she had far too much riding on getting that Hardacre contract. She couldn't afford to let anything derail her plans. Her finger hovered over the reply icon on her screen, but she let her phone drop onto her bed. If she didn't answer, maybe they'd give up and leave her alone. And if they didn't? Would she have to bring this to the attention of the police? There was no actual threat in so many words. Could the police even do anything? She hadn't wanted to bring the whole sorry incident to the police all those years ago and she certainly hadn't changed how she felt about that now.

Yes, she was doing the right thing, she told herself as she grabbed a change of clothes and went into her bathroom. Right now, ignoring *hisgirl* had to be the best option. After a quick shower, Yasmin left her phone where she'd tossed it and returned downstairs.

Ilya was stretched out on a sun lounger by the pool. His body was strong and tanned and healthy with altogether too much flesh on display for her peace of mind. For a second Yasmin wondered what it would have been like to become involved with him outside of the hothouse atmosphere of their arranged marriage. Would they have found compatibility with each other had they met like a regular couple? She mentally shook her head. It was unlikely they'd have interacted at all, except in the most formal manner. Being competition for each other in their field of business, they had everything in common and yet were poles apart at the same time.

And now they were married and had to stay that way until she at least won her contract and saved Carter Air from oblivion. Her gut twisted at the thought of losing her company, but at the same time she hated that it had come to this. That she'd entered into a marriage contract with someone who appeared to be approaching their relationship with every intention of this being a forever thing. And, to be honest, that had been at the back of her mind, too. She hadn't been entirely lying when Ilya had pressed her for her reasons for using Match Made in Marriage, but she certainly hadn't given him the full truth, either.

Being purposely deceitful sat uncomfortably on her shoulders—but, she reminded herself, sometimes you had to walk a fine line.

And if her husband had been anyone other than Ilya…?

She swallowed against the lump that rose in her throat at the thought that right now she could have been on honeymoon with another man. She couldn't fool herself. She doubted very much that another man would appeal to her on the same level Ilya did. He was everything she would have looked for in a husband—if he hadn't been her rival. If their families didn't have that yawning rift between them. If his grandmother hadn't broken her grandfather's heart and made him eventually settle for marriage with a woman he didn't love enough, breaking her heart in the bargain.

But Yasmin was married to Ilya. To the beautiful man right here in front of her. He took off his sunglasses and looked at her now with his sexy, blue eyes in a way that made her feel as though she was wearing nothing at all. He gave her a welcoming smile.

"I was beginning to wonder if you'd decided to take a nap."

"Naps are for old people," Yasmin snorted.

She sat down on the edge of the lounger next to his. The evening sun felt warm through her clothes and on her bare arms and legs.

"Oh, I don't know. Sometimes they're called for. Like those times when you've expended a whole lot of energy and need to restore."

A whole lot of energy? Somehow she didn't think he was talking about their morning hikes in the hills. Her skin prickled.

"I'm going to grab a glass of juice," she said, getting back to her feet. "Can I get you anything?"

"Maybe a beer?"

"I'll be right back."

Yasmin avoided looking at him as she went into the kitchen and got their drinks. But she couldn't erase the image of his near-naked body imprinted on her retinas. Ilya Horvath dressed was hard enough to deal with, but undressed? Her hand shook, making her spill a little of the juice onto the countertop. She cursed under her breath as she reached for a cloth to wipe up the spilled liquid. They didn't even have to be in the same room and she was a mess about him. Something had to give. Maybe she needed to rid herself of the itch that crept under her skin on a daily basis. Maybe she needed to take him up on that offer to share his room when she was ready.

Was she ready? Could she take that step? While it would no doubt assuage some of the perpetual hunger for him that simmered through her body, would it provide relief or would it do more harm than good? Would it cement this orchestrated relationship they had, or would it just make things a whole lot more complicated?

There's only one way to find out, nagged that pesky voice at the back of her mind.

She ignored it and snatched up their drinks, taking them back out to the patio. She put Ilya's beer on the small side table next to his chair, careful to avoid accidentally touching him. Right now she felt so tense with anticipation that she worried what a single touch from him might do.

"Thanks," he said, reaching across for the drink and taking a long pull. "Ah, that's great. Nothing like a cold beer on a hot evening when you've got nothing else to do."

Yasmin sipped her juice, relishing the cold sweetness but wondering if she shouldn't have added a shot of something alcoholic just to take the edge off her nerves. Unfortunately, that brought her back to thinking about the photo she'd just received. It had been years before she'd trusted herself enough to touch alcohol again, and she'd always been a moderate drinker. Now Ilya had her thinking about having a drink.

The man couldn't be good for her. They'd been married a week and already she couldn't get him out of her mind. Going back to work would be a welcome panacea, but that wouldn't happen for another week. She had thought the two-week honeymoon was a good idea at the time. An opportunity to spend time with her new husband and get to know him better.

Know him in the biblical sense? She took another, longer sip of her drink. This was getting ridiculous. Maybe she should just sleep with Ilya and get it over with.

"A penny for your thoughts."

Yasmin felt a blush creep into her cheeks. "Not even worth a penny," she answered dismissively.

"Or you just don't want to tell me," he responded with a little smirk. "I was thinking we could go out for dinner tonight. Maybe the tapas restaurant in town."

A restaurant? That would be good, she thought, nodding in agreement. At least there they would be surrounded by people and maybe, just maybe, she'd stop thinking about how sexy her husband was and what the heck she was going to do about it.

"That sounds great. Would you like me to make the booking? I'm happy to drive us."

"I thought we'd take a car service. That way we can both have a couple of drinks."

And her inhibitions would fly out the window, she thought ruefully. But then, maybe it was time she let them and learned to let go a little. For so long she'd lived such a structured, self-disciplined existence. Get up, work hard, go to bed and then do it all again. Her entire adult life had been one long treadmill of doing the same thing all the time. Working for the greater good of Carter Air and her employees. So why shouldn't she let her hair down and live a little? Especially with a man she was married to.

"Okay," she said, before she could change her mind. "That sounds nice."

Nice? What was she thinking? She wasn't quite sure she was ready to handle this, but then again, she'd never know until she tried, right?

It was late and Ilya couldn't sleep a wink. Dinner had been incredible. The tapas restaurant was always good but somehow sharing the platters with Yasmin had given him a new appetite and enhanced the flavors more than ever.

He'd never met anyone like her before. She was that incredibly perfect blend of beauty and intelligence. And all his life, she'd been living only a short distance away from him. If it hadn't been for that stupid feud between their families, would things have been different? Would they have ever come together under different circumstances, courted like a normal couple and done all the things a regular couple did?

Things like make love under a moonlit sky until they both drifted to sleep in sated exhaustion?

He shifted uncomfortably in his bed. Being around Yasmin was proving very uncomfortable. Not being around her was even worse. Ilya flopped over onto his other side and willed himself to relax, but that was easier said than done when he was once again going to bed with an unrelieved hard-on.

What would she have done, he wondered, if he'd stroked the fine skin of her lightly tanned arms the way he'd wanted to at dinner, or if, when the car had dropped them home, he'd reached over and planted a kiss on the exposed nape of her neck? Would she have shivered in delight? Would she have turned and met his passion with an answering kiss of her own?

He huffed another sigh of frustration. Wherever his thoughts were leading, it was irrelevant. Until Yasmin was ready to come to him on her own terms, he wasn't going to push her. There was still that fragile insecurity beneath the assured surface that she presented to him each morning at breakfast. He wasn't sure why the insecurity was there, or what had created it, but he certainly wasn't going to make it any worse. He could be patient along with the best of them. Even if it just about killed him.

A sound at his door made him stiffen. He opened one eye a crack and detected the svelte silhouette of his wife as she came into the room. Ilya congratulated himself on sleeping with the drapes open, because the weak moonlight provided just enough illumination for him to see his bride step carefully across the room.

She hesitated at the edge of his bed. For a moment he thought she might turn and walk back out as silently as she'd walked in. She'd been incredibly stealthy. If he hadn't been awake and facing the door, he probably wouldn't have heard her arrival. But here she was. An arm's length away. Ilya found himself holding his breath, wondering what she was going to do next.

He didn't have to wait long. Yasmin obviously had made her decision. She reached for the top sheet and slid under it beside him. His body went into overdrive. His every instinct urged him to pull her into his arms and to fulfill the fantasies that had plagued him since he'd left her alone in her bedroom on their wedding night. But he was stronger than that. She could be here for a myriad of reasons—none of them having anything to do with the desperation raging through him right now.

How did a gentleman react in a situation like this? What did he do, or say?

"Bad dream?" he asked gently.

He felt, rather than saw, her shake her head.

"No, nothing like that," she answered. Her voice was husky and she swallowed. "I… I thought it was time I took you up on your offer. I changed my mind about sleeping alone. Are you okay with that?"

Eight

Was he okay with that? *Hell, yes!* He wanted to punch the air and shout out loud.

"Are you certain?" he asked instead.

"I haven't been able to think about anything else. It's…" She hesitated.

"It's…?" he prompted.

"Driving me crazy."

"I have to admit to being a little crazy, too. It's a weird thing, this marriage of ours, isn't it?"

He heard her sigh in the semidarkness. "It really is."

She fell silent beside him. Her body was rigid with tension. Maybe he should have acted on his first instinct after all—gentlemanly conduct be damned. But then he felt her move toward him. Felt a tentative touch of her hand on his shoulder. He reciprocated, letting his hand rest on the curve of her hip. She was wearing some kind of silky slip, and as he stroked her it moved beneath his palm like a luxuriously delicate barrier between them. But as good as it felt, he wanted to feel *her.*

He pushed the fabric higher until he touched bare skin. She wasn't wearing any underwear and the knowledge sent a bolt of heat straight to his groin. His hand shook as he stroked her, pushing the slip higher, feeling the dip of her waist, the shape of her ribs, the curve of her breast. Her breath hitched as he touched her there, as he cupped her fullness and let his thumb drift across her tight nipple.

Her skin was hot, as if she burned with the same need he did. Ilya shifted in the bed so he had better access to her and bent his head to her breast, taking his time kissing and licking a path from the underside to the budded peak. He wished he could see her more clearly. Drink in her beauty, the color of her skin. But like this, in the dark, his other senses became more attuned to her. To the sighs and gasps she made as he caressed her body. To the scent of her—not just the light summery fragrance she wore, but the scent of her body—her desire.

It was a powerful aphrodisiac, the knowledge that she wanted him that much. He continued to lavish attention on her breasts while letting his hand trail down over her taut stomach and lower still. She was obviously the kind of woman who took her personal grooming to the next level, he realized as he felt the tiny neat patch of body hair nestled there. He groaned.

Ah, what he wouldn't do to see that. But there was time. Hopefully tonight would be the first of many such nights where they could explore each other, touch and taste and revel in each other's bodies.

His fingers dipped a little lower, to the molten core of her—slick and soft and, oh, so very tempting. She moved beneath him, a groan coming from her that spoke to how ready she truly was. He let one finger slip inside her and felt her tense and shudder against him.

"You like that?" he asked.

"Oh, yes," she sighed on a quiver of breath. "Don't stop, please."

"Well, since you asked so nicely."

He repeated the movement, this time easing two fingers inside her and curling them to stroke her. Her hips lifted from the bed and she tightened around his fingers again. Keeping his movements small and slow, he continued to caress her, all the while trailing a line of kisses down the center of her body. The scent of her was hot and musky, and yet enticingly sweet, as well. He nuzzled against her mound, pressed a kiss there, then used his tongue to find the pearl hidden in her folds.

Yasmin's hands caught in his hair, holding him to her as he worked his tongue in patterns against her clitoris. Beneath him he felt her body grow more and more tense. It was time. He increased the tempo of his fingers, closed his mouth around her bud and suckled her.

She climaxed on a keening cry, her body shuddering as she came around him, beneath him. It was all he could do not to come himself, such was the force of her orgasm. Instead, he held onto the last shred of his control, determined to make her enjoyment last. His pleasure would come later and be all the better for it.

Ilya slowed his movements, pressed a lingering kiss against her and withdrew his fingers from her body.

"I know this probably comes across as cliché," she said, her voice just a little shaky. "But wow."

Ilya laughed, loving the fact that she could make a joke at a time like this.

"I've yet to meet the man who wouldn't find that a compliment," he admitted, still smiling.

He lay down next to her and pulled her closer to him.

"I meant it as one," she answered, pressing a kiss against his shoulder. "And now, it's your turn."

"There's no need—"

"Shush, there's every need. I'm all about equal opportunities. Aren't you?" she teased.

She nipped him and the sensation of her teeth against his skin sent another jolt of desire crashing through him. He'd be lucky to hold on another minute, let alone for as long as she planned to torture him. And torture it was. Sweet, delicious, sensation-filled torture as she explored his body with her hands, her lips and her tongue.

Every now and then her hand would drift close to his groin and brush against his penis, making it twitch involuntarily. His balls were so tight they ached, and the pleasurable pain of it nearly drove him to distraction. Tremors began to rock him as she worked her way down his body, as her teeth scraped over the sensitive skin at the V of his groin. If she was going to do that somewhere else, he—

She did. Ilya clenched his fists in the sheets beside him, allowed his body to ride the wave of sheer unadulterated pleasure that threatened to swamp him. Her fingers closed around his shaft, stroking him as she took his tip deeper into her mouth. It was too much. Far, far, far too much.

In one swift movement, Ilya pulled her up higher on his body.

"You're killing me," he barely uttered as he lifted her over his engorged shaft and slowly lowered her down.

"You didn't let me finish."

"Oh, we'll finish. I promise."

As her body engulfed him, he closed his eyes and gritted his teeth, calling on every last ounce of restraint. This wasn't about him anymore. It was about both of them. Together.

His hips began to move and Yasmin met him, thrust for thrust. He could just make her out in the low gleam of moonlight from the window. Her slender body was rising and falling—undulating like waves on the sea. His climax was near, but he had to be certain she was going to fall over that edge with him. He fought the urge to give in. Felt her body grow tight around him, felt the rhythmic pull of her orgasm beginning.

He could hold on no longer. She was his absolute undoing. He let go, riding the intense swell of pleasure, again and again. And she let go with him, her body tensing and releasing on her own waves of delight, until she collapsed over him.

Ilya wrapped his arms about her, felt the last tiny tremors course through her body before she went completely slack in his arms.

"Yeah, wow," he murmured into her hair.

"I can't move," she said languidly. "You're going to have to push me off."

"I kind of like having you right here," he replied, closing his arms a little tighter and relishing the feel of her body against his.

Her breath came in short little puffs of warm air against his chest and he felt her body relax as she sank into sleep in his arms.

He'd never thought it could be like this. The depths of passion, the heights of satisfaction, the closeness of remaining joined when he finally lost hold on consciousness and drifted into a satiated sleep himself.

It was still dark when Yasmin woke. She remained sprawled over Ilya's chest, her legs splayed on either side of his. Her entire body hummed with a sense of completion she'd never known before. A part of her wondered why the heck she'd waited so long to give in to the attraction that had driven her crazy this past week. The other part told her she was simply being careful.

This changed things. Making love to Ilya had taken their marriage to a new level of permanence for her. Had it been the same for him? She gave a little shiver as she remembered the things he'd done, the reactions he'd wrought from her. She was no shy violet in the bedroom but he'd brought her to the precipice of something new and exciting. Something she knew would be addictive.

Was she ready to do this? To give herself over to that level of commitment? They'd known each other and been married just a week. It was all kinds of madness to be feeling this way so soon. He was her enemy in business and yet, here in his bed, she knew he was anything but.

Was this the real Ilya Horvath? A man who rescued puppies? A man who saw to her every daily need? A man who reduced her to a puddle of loose limbs and fulfillment after just one sexual encounter?

So where did this leave her? Confused, yes. Wanting more, most definitely.

But did Ilya feel the same way? How did a girl go about asking a man something like that?

"You're thinking too hard," Ilya said sleepily from beneath her.

His voice rumbled in her ear. His hand, which only moments ago had rested limply on the small of her back, now began to drift gently, tracing the knobs of her spine. Up and down and back up again.

"Is that even possible, to think too hard?"

"It is when you should be sleeping or making love."

Desire unfurled in her like petals opening on a full-blown rose.

"And which would you suggest in this instance?" she asked, lifting her head and looking at his face.

His eyes glinted in the dark.

"The latter, of course."

"Is that so? Didn't you have enough the first time around?"

He shook his head. "That was only a starter to whet your appetite. Did I fail?"

She laughed at the mock mortification in his tone.

"No, you didn't fail. But, then again, I don't expect you know what that's like."

His hand stilled on her back. "You think I've never failed?"

"Have you?"

"Enough to know what it feels like," he said grimly. "But I don't want to talk about that right now. Right now, I'd rather do this."

He rolled them over so she was beneath him, and he settled between her thighs. She could feel his arousal, already hard and heavy, probing at her entrance.

He hesitated. "We didn't discuss contraception," he said, his voice blunt.

"I get the birth control shot. And I know we're both clean. It was one of the tests we had to have before the wedding, remember?"

She flexed a little, felt the tip of him enter her. She gasped on a flood of awareness.

"Too soon?" he asked, nuzzling the curve of her neck.

"Not soon enough," she replied, pushing her pelvis forward so she could take him in farther.

He withdrew teasingly. "Oh, I don't know."

She dug her fingernails into his buttocks and felt him flinch.

"Not soon enough," she repeated.

"Then I had best continue as the lady demands," he said, punctuating his sentence with a thrust of his hips.

"That's more like it," Yasmin sighed in approval.

"I aim to please."

"There's nothing whatsoever wrong with your aim," she managed to say before ripples of desire built up inside her and threatened to sweep away any capacity to speak.

This time her climax was deeper, more intense than before, and she knew, through every step, that Ilya was with her all the way. When he came she felt it through her whole body, her pleasure and his mixing and blending and radiating through them until they were both left spent and breathing heavily.

She'd known pleasure and satisfaction before, but nothing—*nothing*—came close to this. Boneless, sated beyond belief, she drifted back into a deep sleep, oblivious to the screen on her mobile phone on the nightstand next to her, lighting up with an incoming email notification.

Nine

He hadn't expected it to be like this, Ilya thought as he and Yasmin walked hand in hand along the beach the next day. They'd driven out to the coast. Feeling the salt air buffet them as the wind whipped down the sandy shoreline and watching the huge breakers roll in, Ilya felt as though the landscape was a fine analogy for the turmoil that churned inside him.

He certainly hadn't expected this depth of connection with another person so quickly. Oh, sure, he knew a lot of how he was feeling was due to their incredible sexual connection. What man wouldn't feel bonded to a woman who made him feel the way Yasmin did when they made love? But it went deeper than that, and that knowledge scared him.

He'd loved a woman before. Believed, with every

cell in his body, that she was The One. Yes, they'd been young, but there was no rule saying young people couldn't love each other forever, was there? Although, in their case, forever had only lasted three years. When he'd discovered that the Jennifer he'd fallen in love with had been a fake, that the true woman beneath the smiles, the affection, the plans for the future had, in fact, been a cruel, lying and scheming bitch, the damage to his heart had been total.

Ilya was the kind of man who, once he committed to something or someone, did it totally and utterly. And he'd committed himself to her. Discovering her web of lies had been shattering—not only to his heart but to his very belief system. His trust in himself, his ability to judge others, had been damaged, and in every relationship since, he'd held a part of himself back—unwilling or unable to go that extra distance to commit to another person.

He knew all about heartbreak. The loss of his father and then his mom in his teens had almost brought him to his knees. Nagy had been his foundation through those years. His rock. His stability. And when she'd seen him off to college, she'd encouraged him to find himself and to test his place in the world. When he met Jennifer at a rival college game, he'd honestly thought she was the woman he would grow old with, and discovering her true nature had been as wrenching as a bereavement. It had made him hard—he knew that, accepted it—because being hard meant being invincible. The only trouble was that he could already feel the cracks forming in his carefully constructed walls. And opening yourself to another person meant opening yourself to hurt.

He'd thought full emotional engagement wouldn't be necessary in his unconventional marriage. That loyalty, kindness and devotion would be enough. But the way his feelings were developing for Yasmin was taking him on a roller-coaster ride he wasn't sure he was ready for.

"Shall we go and sit over there, out of the wind?" Yasmin asked, interrupting his thoughts and gesturing to a hollow between a couple of low sand hills.

"Sure." He tucked her hand into the crook of his arm as they ploughed through the loose sand and settled in the spot she'd indicated.

"It's so gorgeous here, so different from the valley. But it looks better from the air," she commented.

"Are you missing flying? We can go to the airfield if you're suffering withdrawal."

"I could take you up in the Ryan if you like," she offered after a short silence.

He felt his pulse kick up a beat. Her Ryan was her pride and joy from what he knew. He admired the amount of time she had to have spent with her grandfather on its restoration. A project like that was a true labor of love. He also knew that she would be in command of the controls and that was something he struggled with. Not because she was a woman, but because ever since his father's death Ilya had rarely relinquished being the pilot in command. Even on commercial airliners he struggled with the concept of someone else being in charge. These days, in most cases, he flew one of the company jets when traveling long haul, even when he went to Europe or to any of the Pacific Islands for a break. He wasn't rated to fly anything like the Ryan, though, so Yasmin would be at the controls, meaning a complete surrender of his instinct to remain in charge.

"You don't have to if you don't want to," she said hastily when he didn't reply. "It's not everyone's cup of tea."

"It's not that."

"You're a control freak, I know. I get it."

Did she? Did she really understand? How could anyone know what it was like to know you faced certain death if you didn't get everything one hundred percent right and that the only person you could trust or rely on was yourself?

"A control freak?" he asked. "Do I come across that way to you?"

"It's possible you're hiding your true nature," she surmised, looking up at him and smiling.

"Humph," he grunted.

"Are you? Hiding your true nature, that is? I know we've been on best behavior with each other since the wedding. It's like we're living in an artificial bubble, really. Don't you think so?"

"That's one way of looking at it, I guess. But, in answer to your question, I'm not hiding my true nature from you. I am what I am. The man you see right here, right now."

She reached up to kiss him. "I'm finding you surprisingly okay for a Horvath. Who knew?"

He laughed. "Yeah, that old family feud thing."

She started to say something but stopped when his cell phone began to chime. He pulled it from his pocket and checked the caller ID.

"It's Danni," he said and thumbed the screen to accept the call.

Yasmin squirmed beside him as he listened to his cousin, keeping his responses to a minimum. When he ended the call he looked at his wife.

"Well?" she demanded.

"We can pick him up later today. If you still want him, that is."

She punched him on his upper arm. "Want him? He's ours. Of course I want him. What are you waiting for?"

She stood up abruptly, leaving him in a shower of sand falling from her jeans. He swiftly followed suit and they laughingly raced each other back along the beach to where they'd parked. As they reached the car, he caught Yasmin's eye across the roof and sent her a smile, realizing, with a small measure of shock, just how much it made him happy to make her happy, as well. Which brought him back to his original turmoil.

No, this connection, this sense of belonging with another person—it wasn't what he'd expected at all.

They were curled up on the large L-shaped couch in the family room, watching the puppy sleep in his crate. The floor was strewn with his toys and puppy pee pads, although Ilya suspected they wouldn't need those as the dog already appeared to have been toilet trained somewhere along the line. Danni suspected he was between three and four months old and a mix of border collie and who knew what else. They had yet to name him.

"He's so cute when he's sleeping, isn't he?" Yasmin commented.

"You said the same when he was awake."

"Well, he's cute. Don't you think so?"

Ilya studied the little guy. They'd been surprised to discover that, once cleaned up, he had quite a bit of white hair interspersed with the patches of brown and black. "Sure, he is."

"I think we should call him Blaze, for the white blaze down his face."

"Yeah, that fits."

"Good. He has a home and a name."

"What are we going to do with him when we go back to work?" Ilya asked.

"I can take him with me."

"And when you're flying?"

"My office manager will look after him…or you could."

"Ah, yes, take-your-dog-to-work day. It has a certain ring to it." He shuddered visibly.

"You're teasing me," she said, struggling to disentangle herself from where she was nestled comfortably against his side.

"Of course I'm teasing you. We'll work something out. Besides, there's always Hannah or doggy day care. Danni mentioned one not too far from here."

"Well, I guess if she recommended it…" Yasmin's voice trailed off.

It occurred to Ilya that his wife had trust issues similar to his own, especially when it came to what was important to her. He wondered what was behind it, although being dumped by your parents on a cantankerous grandparent probably had something to do with it.

The house phone began to ring and Ilya reluctantly rose from the couch to answer it. His grandmother was the only person who called his landline anymore, and he had no doubt she was calling to check on the state of his marriage.

"I expected you to have rung me by now," she said imperiously the moment he answered the phone. "Why aren't you still up in Port Ludlow?"

"I've been busy getting to know my wife. You know, the one you paired me with? And besides, we wanted to come home. When did you find out?"

Of all the cousins, he was always the one who got away with the most with Nagy. None of the others would dare be as cheeky.

"When and how I found out is neither here nor there. Is all going well?" she asked, blithely ignoring his dig.

He looked over at Yasmin, who was flicking through a sports aviation magazine she'd picked up off the coffee table.

"As well as can be expected."

"Oh, for goodness sake, Ilya! Stop beating around the bush."

"I don't know what you mean," he teased.

"Would you like me to visit, then?"

There was a steeliness to his grandmother's voice

that left him in no doubt that she would breach the family's agreement to leave the newlyweds to themselves during the honeymoon period.

"You know you're always welcome, but in this case, I think we should leave it a while. You can be assured that my wife and I—" he paused to smile at Yasmin who'd looked up at that point "—are getting on very well and enjoying learning more about each other. Oh, and we have a puppy."

"A dog? Already?" His grandmother sounded flabbergasted. "Well, that's quick."

"We found him when we were out on a walk in the hills. Danni brought him back to health for us. You'll love him."

"That remains to be seen. You know how I feel about animals."

"Was there anything else, Nagy?"

"No, you go back to your wife. And Ilya?" She paused.

"Yes."

"I know you two can make this work."

She hung up without saying goodbye, but he was used to that. She never wasted time on small talk. It was one of the many things he respected about her.

He settled on the couch again and pulled Yasmin back under his arm. He liked the way she fit there. In fact, he liked the way she fit in his life, period. And despite its being what he should have wanted in a relationship, it still made him uneasy because he wasn't ready to fully let her in—to his mind or his heart.

* * *

Alice hung up the phone and allowed a small smile to play across her face. It was working—better than she'd hoped, in fact. She hadn't been wrong yet with her pairings, but it was always reassuring to know she hadn't lost her touch.

A puppy? She smiled again, a small chuckle bubbling up from deep inside. Her first-born grandson was actually settling down. She'd begun to fear it would never happen. He'd been so shy of commitment since that awful eye-opening time back in college. Oh, sure. He had a beautiful home in the hills fit for a family. He had money socked away for a rainy day. He had a satisfying career and more family support than a man could ever need. But she knew he'd only been going through the motions these past ten or more years.

When her Ilya gave, he gave everything. Having that love, that trust, abused by a gold-digging, lying piece of… She shut down her thoughts before rage could take over and trigger another of those blasted angina attacks that only she and her doctor knew about. Alice calmed her breathing, cleared her mind and allowed herself to only think about what made her happiest. Family.

Her earnest boy, her knight crusader, was finally learning to give of that most precious part of himself, his heart. She only hoped she'd done the right thing because she knew, without doubt, that if his heart was given and, perish the thought, broken again, nothing would repair it.

Ten

Yasmin walked around the Ryan doing her pre-flight checks. It felt a bit strange to be at the airport and not go into the office. Her plane was hangared separately from the Carter Air charter planes, but Riya had threatened her with all kinds of harm if she so much as set foot in the office before her official honeymoon period came to an end.

Riya might be small, but she was a force to be reckoned with, and while Yasmin's instinct was just to pop in and check on things, she didn't want to incur her friend's wrath. If there was a serious problem, Riya would let her know. Besides, if Ilya could stay away from his work for two weeks, then she could most definitely do the same.

Excitement bubbled in her veins. She hadn't flown

since before the wedding and she was itching to get behind the controls and dance across the sky. And Ilya was coming up with her. He'd surprised her this morning, on their last Friday before they went back to work, saying he'd decided to take her up on her offer of the flight in the old trainer. Hannah was minding Blaze for them and Yasmin was thrilled at the idea of taking her husband up and showing off a little. But even more important, he was showing her he trusted her, which was pretty incredible, given his own admitted preference to be the pilot in command.

The only shadow on her day was the latest email on her phone. The words had burned themselves into her memory, leaving her wondering who on earth from her past *hisgirl* could be. It obviously had to be someone from her time in college—the photo suggested as much—but she'd ceased to have contact with any of them after that humiliating night.

If you know what's good for you, you'll walk out of his life and never go back.

The inherent threat had made her blood run cold, especially on the heels of the photo *hisgirl* had sent earlier in the week. Was the sender specifically warning her that if she didn't leave Ilya the photo would be used against her somehow?

Perhaps it was someone Ilya had gone out with, but then, how would that person have access to photos taken at the hazing? And what on earth did they hope to gain by threatening Yasmin? If Ilya had been invested in a relationship with anyone else, he wouldn't have put himself in his grandmother's hands for a Match Made in Marriage arrangement. He wasn't that kind of guy.

Her head ached the more she thought about it. The only thing she knew for certain was that there were far more questions than answers. She'd decided to ask Ilya if he'd been seeing anyone prior to marrying her, but the opportunity hadn't arisen. Or maybe she was just too scared to bring it up in case he pressed her for reasons why she was asking.

She trailed a hand along the leading edge of the wing and, putting all her confusion aside, completed her preflight inspection.

Ilya was waiting for her beside the plane. "All good?"

"As it should be," she replied with a smile. "You're ready?"

"When it comes to flying, and some other things, come to think of it, I'm definitely ready," he said with a smile that made her stomach flip and her legs turn to jelly.

She growled at herself to pull her act together and focus on the flight plan she'd created for today. "All right then," Yasmin said. "We'd better climb aboard."

The airport was less busy than usual and the tower quickly gave Yasmin clearance to take off. In no time they were taxiing down the runway, engine noise filling the open cockpit. Yasmin keyed her mic.

"You doing okay?"

"I'm not having to sit on my hands to stop myself from touching the controls just yet, so, yeah, I'm fine."

She laughed. She could only imagine how he'd be feeling right now in the front seat of the plane. Visibility wasn't that great while taxiing in the tail-dragger, but once they were airborne? Well, that would be a different story altogether.

Yasmin felt the tail lift off and experienced the accompanying thrill she always got when she took the Ryan up. A few seconds later they were climbing out. She reached her chosen altitude and keyed the mic again.

"I'm going to take her through a few maneuvers. Hold on to your stomach!"

He gave her a thumbs-up and she pushed the plane into a gentle roll.

"Is that all you got?" he taunted once she'd righted the plane again. "C'mon, I know you have more tricks up your sleeve."

"You asked for it," she said, taking up the challenge.

The aerobatic sequence she did was one she often performed at air shows, and the exhilaration was no less for having an enthusiastic passenger on board. But as she came out of a stall and into a spin she wondered if she was taking things a step too far. After all, Ilya was a self-confessed autocrat when it came to being in a cockpit. It wouldn't feel natural to him to be in the front passenger seat and not take the controls, especially when it felt as though the plane might plummet to the ground any second.

Maneuvers completed, she leveled out and flew out

toward the coast. There was something about watching the sea from the air that always calmed her, no matter what kind of day she was having. Her headset crackled to life.

"That. Was. Amazing."

Her lips curved into a grateful smile. "I'm glad you enjoyed it."

"Seriously, you're a brilliant pilot."

Yasmin felt her chest swell with pride. She didn't often hear praise so heartfelt, and having it come from Ilya? Well, that just made it all the more special.

"Do you want to fly her for a bit?" she asked. "Nothing too fancy, but just to have a taste of how she handles."

"Hell, yeah."

Yasmin ran through a few of the basics, underscoring some of the touchier tendencies of the aircraft. "You have control," she said after Ilya relayed the details back to her to indicate he'd understood.

Her heart shuddered a little in her chest. Since rebuilding the Ryan with her grandfather, she was the only person to have ever flown the aircraft. Giving control to Ilya now was the deepest mark of respect and trust she'd ever shown anyone. And doing so felt completely natural to her, which came as another shock. Tomorrow, they'd have been married two weeks. How on earth had she, the quintessential distrustful soul, as Riya called her, come so far in this relationship already that she was prepared to relinquish control of her greatest pride and joy? She rubbed at her chest, at the lump that had settled there. Was this what falling in love was like?

She hadn't counted on this feeling. Didn't quite know how to handle it. Marrying Ilya—well, whoever would have been waiting at the altar for her, to be honest—had merely been a means to an end. A solution to a problem that had grown beyond her ability to manage. Developing feelings like this for him so soon? It was ridiculous, she told herself firmly. People didn't fall in love that quickly.

But they did, her conscience whispered. Hadn't her parents met and fallen and love and married all within the space of a few weeks? Hadn't they always said that they'd known, the moment they'd laid eyes on each other, that it was meant to be and they shouldn't waste another moment beating around the bush and following courtship rituals when they could simply begin their lives together immediately? And even Riya, whose marriage had been arranged by her family back in India, had only met her husband a handful of times before they married. When Yasmin had mentioned how archaic she felt the concept of arranged marriage was, Riya had simply smiled in contentment and told her that *When you know, you just know.*

Did Yasmin know? Not for certain. *So, let's look at this logically*, she told herself. *Despite your reasons for marrying, you're married to a guy who is very likely every straight woman's dream of perfection. He isn't the overbearing jerk you heard he was. In fact, he's nothing like that. In many ways, he's a lot like you. Focused. Businesslike. Ready to start a family. To carry on a legacy.*

Yasmin stared unseeingly at the coastline that zipped along beneath them, not liking the direction of her thoughts.

"I think we should head back now," she said abruptly.

"She's all yours," came Ilya's voice through the headset.

Yasmin took the control column in her hand and turned the plane back to the airport, completing a textbook-perfect landing and taxiing back to the hangar. She'd no sooner completed her routine of putting the Ryan to bed, as she called it, when Ilya wrapped his strong arms around her from behind and spun her around. In the next instant he was kissing her as if his life depended on it. If this was how he reacted when she took him up with her, she'd have to do it more often.

Desire for him flamed hot and fast through her veins and she gave back every bit as good as he was giving her. It was only when she realized that her hands were at his shirtfront, her fingers feverishly plucking at his buttons, that she came to her senses.

"Not here. My apartment. Upstairs."

She grabbed his hand and tugged him out the back door to the external stairs that led to her grandfather's old apartment. She'd made it her own after he died, not seeing the point in paying rent anywhere else. Its proximity to work couldn't be faulted. Right now, though, proximity to a bed was uppermost in her mind as she led Ilya up the stairs. His feet hammered on the steps behind her and her blood was pumping fast when she fitted her key in the lock and pulled the door open.

The second they were inside she turned and pushed Ilya against the door, kissing him with all the hunger she'd bottled up since he'd kissed her in the hangar. They shed their clothing, leaving it in scattered heaps as they made their way to her bedroom. Seconds later, they tumbled onto her mattress in a tangle of limbs. She straddled him and their joining was fast and heated, her climax coming so quickly it shocked the air from her lungs and left her in a state of limbo between pleasure and unconsciousness before she felt Ilya shudder in completion beneath her.

His hands pulled her down to him and he rolled them onto their sides. Now he faced her with a silly grin. His breathing was about as irregular as hers and she put her hand out, flattening her palm against his bare chest, feeling the erratic beat of his heart that matched her own.

"Is this where I say *wow*?" he asked, his voice uneven.

"Yeah, this would be a good time," she answered, as breathless as if she'd just completed a half marathon.

"Wow."

Yasmin laughed, the sound gurgling up from deep inside her and taking her over. Joy filled her from the soles of her feet upward. Ilya joined her, and together they lay there, laughing like a pair of idiots on her bed. Eventually she calmed, lacing her fingers through his.

"Is this what you're always like when you relinquish control?" she laughed, squeezing his hand.

"I could get used to it," he admitted with a rueful expression on his handsome face.

"We should do this more often," she said. "Go flying together, I mean. Although the rest was pretty good, too."

"I couldn't agree more." He rolled flat onto his back. "Thank you."

"For the sex?" she teased.

"For everything. I didn't know how I'd feel not being the pilot in command."

His voice trailed off, and Yasmin heard him sigh deeply.

"It wasn't as bad as I thought," he said on a huff of breath. "In fact, it was pretty damn incredible. *You're* pretty damn incredible—and fearless."

Yasmin felt his praise roll through her and savored it. It had been a long time since anyone had told her she'd done well.

"Thanks. I'm glad it was okay for you. I… I understand what it can be like facing your fears. But I would never say I'm fearless. I have plenty of fears—in fact, I could barely stand to put my head under water until a few years ago—but flying…no, that isn't one of them."

She traced little circles on his chest with a finger, enjoying the fact that they could lie here together so comfortably with no urgency to leave. She felt the vibrations of his voice when he spoke.

"Tell me about your biggest fear, then. Maybe we can get you over it, since you've apparently cured me of needing to be the boss all the time."

Should she tell him? Could she? Even though they were husband and wife they essentially remained strangers to each other. Yasmin had never told another soul about that night—about her desperation to fit in and belong with the in-crowd at college. Why she'd even let it be so important to her back then still embarrassed her.

"Yasmin?" he prompted.

She drew in a deep breath, made a decision. She had nothing to fear from Ilya, did she?

"My biggest fear is not being able to see. To be blindfolded, to have all vision restricted and be led into a situation so dangerous it almost kills you—" She paused and let go a deep breath. "Yeah, that's my greatest fear."

Ilya stiffened beneath her touch as her words sank in. Coupled with that sense of having seen Yasmin somewhere in his past, somewhere outside of the rare times they'd run across each other at industry affairs, the mention of a blindfold and almost being killed dragged him back to a time he'd chosen to push to the back of his memories.

"Almost kills you?" he asked, seeking confirmation that she was indeed talking about the incident he thought she was.

"I guess I should tell you everything," Yasmin said, withdrawing her hand from his.

She sat up in the bed, pulled her knees up against her chest and wrapped her arms around her legs, making herself seem smaller. Ilya reached up and traced his fingers down her spine, determined to ensure that she didn't feel alone in this.

"Only tell me if you're ready," he coaxed gently.

"I'm ready. It's just that I've never trusted anyone enough to share this before."

"Are you worried I'll use it against you somehow?"

"Oh, heavens, no! I—" She stopped and drew in a breath. "I just wouldn't want you to think of me any differently, y'know? Because of what happened."

"Why don't you let me be the judge of that," he said cautiously.

"Fine," she said with a broken little smile that scored at his heart. "All my life I'd worked so hard to be the best student and athlete I could be. I guess a part of that was the hope that if I proved to my parents that I was a really good kid, they might come back and we'd live as a family again. When I realized it didn't matter what I did, they were never coming back, I constantly sought my grandfather's approval. It took a lot to impress him."

She laughed. It was a bitter sound that lacked any humor, and it made Ilya angry at the old man all over again. Yasmin had deserved better than that.

She continued, lost in her memories. "Because I was so driven, I never made close friends at school. When I wasn't studying, I was training, when I wasn't training, I was competing or helping Granddad out at the airfield. So when it came to fitting in at college I was determined to be just like everyone else. It's ridiculous how hard I worked to be normal," she said, making air quotes as she spoke the last word. "I was prepared to do anything to fit in. Anything."

Ilya felt his skin crawl with damning inevitability as she mentioned where she'd gone to college. The same college as Jennifer. He wanted desperately to reassure her. To tell her that she was normal, that she'd always been. That it had been the others who weren't. But doing so would be admitting to his own involvement, his own shame.

"When I tried to join the most popular sorority, the hazing was intense. The final test was held at a secluded lakeside beach after midnight. The list of challenges was extensive, and involved drinking a lot of alcohol if I did or said anything wrong. I've never been much of a drinker and the vodka shots hit me hard. I ended up doing things I would never have done sober but I was desperate to fit in—to be a part of something other kids my age did as a matter of course. I was already pretty drunk when they blindfolded me and told me I had to swim off the beach to a diving pontoon and then back to the beach again. Any normal day I would have done that without any trouble, but with all that alcohol in my system it didn't end well. I nearly drowned. I failed the challenge and someone, I don't even know who, had to pull me out of the water.

"I ended up in the hospital emergency room getting my stomach pumped and being put on IV fluids to sober me up. It was the most shameful experience of my life. I'll never forget the lecture the ER doctor gave me. Of course I didn't make it into the sorority and I was shunned by the girls I'd so pathetically wanted to be my friends. It was a tough lesson but I took it on the chin. I transferred back home and finished my degree at Cal State and carried on with my life. But it left its scars, you know? I conquered the fear of swimming that it gave me, but I still can't bear to have my eyes covered or lose my eyesight in any way. It totally freaks me out."

He could well believe it.

"And you've never told anyone? You didn't report it to the college administration?"

He already knew the answer, but he didn't understand why she'd chosen not to report the people involved.

"How could I? I chose to participate and I did some pretty disgusting things, again by choice. I could have walked away, given up at any time like a few other girls did when the challenges started getting too bizarre. Some of the kids there took photos that night." Her voice caught on a hitch. "I was warned that if I said anything, those pictures might come out. I couldn't have borne that. It was easier to leave than to be judged for what I'd done."

How on earth could she feel as if she would be judged for what happened that night? She'd been the victim and then blackmailed into the bargain. As if all of that hadn't been bad enough, his then-fiancée had been the bully behind it all.

He couldn't believe that Yasmin was the one he'd pulled from the water that night. Looking at her now, it was difficult to reconcile the slender, blond and competent woman he was getting to know with the broken girl he'd hauled out. She'd been considerably plumper then, her hair long and much darker—more a shade of brown than the blond it was now. She looked completely different now, unrecognizable. He'd never heard her name spoken that night or known who she was. He'd only known she was in trouble and needed rescuing. So he'd saved her.

At the time Jennifer had begged him not to call the authorities. She'd promised that the girl would be looked after and convinced him that what had happened was simply a silly prank that had gotten out of hand—that there was nothing malicious in it.

Saying nothing had gone against everything he'd ever been taught about right and wrong and he'd been furious with Jen. But she was his fiancée. He'd loved her. He planned to have a life together with her. He had to believe her, trust in her, didn't he? And he had, right up until the moment a few days later when he'd overheard Jen boasting about the hazing and laughing about how he'd spoiled her fun. That had been the moment his eyes had opened and he'd realized that his friends, who'd said early on in their relationship that she was using him, were right about her. He could never spend the rest of his life with a woman as callous and as cruel as that.

He'd been a fool and, at that point, the person he had lost most faith in was himself.

Looking at Yasmin through new eyes, he realized he wanted to save her now, too. Save her from the dreadful guilt she still carried for her part in that night.

He was desperate to reassure Yasmin, but for the first time in his life words completely failed him. How could he tell her he had been there that night, though not until after she'd entered the water? How could he tell her how he'd been linked to the woman who'd put her through hell? Whose actions, even now, continued to have an impact on Yasmin's life?

At the same time, he was in shock himself. His *wife* was the woman he'd rescued from the water that truly awful night. Was it some crazy coincidence or had his grandmother somehow known about the incident? She'd orchestrated their union. Was this some twisted idea of hers, pairing him and Yasmin now? It wouldn't surprise him. She'd always had an uncanny instinct when it came to others and when he'd returned home to tell her in person about his broken engagement she hadn't pressed him for details. She'd only offered her sympathy and told him that she trusted he would always do the right thing. He itched to grill her on the subject now, but that would have to be a discussion for another time. Right now, he had to reassure Yasmin that she had done nothing wrong. Her fear was a direct result of what others had done to her that night and she herself was not responsible.

If he'd acted then as he should have, and reported the whole sorry situation to the college, it would have been handled appropriately. And Yasmin wouldn't have had to bear the guilt she continued to carry to this very day. It was too late now. He couldn't undo the past. But he could help Yasmin in the future.

He'd told himself he was committed to their marriage—now he had to prove he was committed to her.

Eleven

He owed it to Yasmin, he told himself. If he couldn't or wouldn't take that chance, then he had no business being married to her at all. And right now, her openness, her honesty, deserved a response. He pushed himself upright and gathered her in his arms, pulling her body to his and offering her comfort. Too little too late, he realized, as he chose his words carefully. But he had to start somewhere.

"You're being too hard on yourself. From what you've told me, it's clear you were never to blame. Not for any of it."

She shook her head and he put his hands on either side of her face, tilting it up to look her in the eye.

"Trust me, Yasmin. I know what I'm talking about.

You put your faith in the wrong people, that's all. What came next was out of your control."

Tears shone in her eyes and a spear of guilt shafted through him. He hated that this strong, proud woman was still so wounded by that night. Somehow, he had to make it right. Had to restore her to her full strength and heal the pain her experience had left behind.

"You're not to blame," he said emphatically.

Her lower lip trembled and one tear formed a silvery trail down her cheek. He'd never been able to cope with a woman's tears and seeing his proud wife crumble like this was absolutely his undoing. He captured her lips with his and tried to imbue that kiss with all of his admiration for her. For her courage, for her talent as a pilot, for her determination to put the past behind her and to stride forward with the life she'd chosen. When they broke apart he stared straight into her eyes. Her pupils were dilated with the desire that burned like an eternal flame between them.

"You're not to blame," he repeated.

He made love to her then. Slowly, intensely. Taking his time to explore her body, to discover every hidden pleasure point, to learn and imprint her in his mind, to make her understand just how much he admired her, how much he wanted her. He renewed his fascination with the silky texture of her skin, the essential flavor of her. And when he entered her he felt a stronger connection to her than before. A connection that thrilled and terrified him in equal proportions. When they reached the pinnacle of satisfaction, they did so together, tumbling into the abyss of pleasure and satiation with a joy that took his breath away.

She dozed in the aftermath, securely nestled against him. But Ilya couldn't rest. His mind twisted and churned over the facts. Over his involvement. She deserved to know it all. She blamed herself for everything but his judgment had also been lacking—after all, hadn't he believed himself in love with Jen? Believed her when she'd said things had gotten out of control when what happened had been part of her plan for Yasmin all along? He should have known better.

He didn't want secrets between Yasmin and himself, but how could he tell her without destroying the fragile beauty of their growing closeness? These past two weeks had been an exercise in learning about one another, about developing trust. Would telling her shatter all of that? She'd been so brave telling him about what had happened, he feared disclosing his involvement with her nemesis would crush any chance they had of continuing to build this marriage of theirs.

He pulled her more firmly against him, breathing in her subtle fragrance and relishing the sensation of her bare skin against his. Savoring the trust she'd imbued in him with her words today. He owed it to her to tell her and he would, eventually, but the timing had to be right. He had to be sure that in doing so he wouldn't push her away from him forever. And, in the meantime, he'd do his best to show her every single day how important she had become to him.

* * *

Ilya felt an unexpected listlessness as they drove back home to the hills. Today had been a revelation for him in more ways than one. Not only had she opened up to him—which had been a gift in itself, even though it had opened a whole new can of worms—but she'd been the instrument that had made him face his own need to constantly be in charge and, more importantly, to learn when to relinquish control. She'd opened his eyes in a way he hadn't believed possible. There was a freedom in trusting others—a lightness in his chest that had been missing for a very long time. That it was his arranged wife who'd introduced him to the concept was a complete about-face from the self-sufficiency he'd prided himself on for most of his life.

He was glad they'd stopped at her apartment. Not only because of the pleasure they'd found in each other while they were there, but because it gave him another window into Yasmin's life. Her apartment was furnished comfortably but sparsely, with an eye for function rather than beauty. He doubted she ever had spent any more time there than absolutely necessary. In fact, there was so little of *her* in the apartment, aside from the occasional photo of an aircraft on the wall, that if he hadn't known her as well as he was learning to, he would have thought her dull, boring, uninspired.

His body tightened on a memory of exactly how inspired she truly was as he remembered their love-making. No, her apartment was not a reflection of her at all. Unless it served as a reminder of her ability to compartmentalize her life. She was a conundrum, this wife of his. More at home in an aircraft than in a car. Happiest throwing said aircraft around the sky than making a house or apartment feel like a home. And there were so many more facets to her still to discover, he told himself as they turned into the driveway.

But opening her up, getting to understand her better, meant opening himself up more to her, too. Putting himself in the line of fire, giving her the power to hurt him. If that was the case, his rational mind argued, didn't he have the power to hurt her also? He rejected the idea. Hurting Yasmin was not an option. But getting to know her better, to understand exactly what made her tick, that most definitely was.

Blaze greeted them exuberantly from inside his crate when they let themselves into the house. Ilya took him outside to do his business in the garden while Yasmin took the clothes she'd brought from her apartment upstairs to their room. She was back downstairs in no time.

"Hungry?" she asked as Ilya walked back to the patio with the puppy bounding along beside him.

"Ravenous. Someone gave me a workout today."

"Aerobatics will do that to a person," she answered flippantly.

"I'm not talking about the aerobatics. At least, not the ones in the air."

Her pupils dilated and a flush lit her cheeks. For a few seconds they were both thrown back into the memory of the passion they'd shared. But then Blaze yipped, breaking the spell. Yasmin bent to give the puppy her attention.

"Hannah told me she'd leave a roasted vegetable salad and steaks for our meal tonight," she said after giving Blaze a good rub that had him rolling onto his back in pleasure. "Do you want to do the meat on the grill?"

"Sure."

It was all so normal, so domesticated, and he liked it. A lot. They walked into the kitchen together, the puppy trotting along beside them. This was the life he'd told himself he always wanted and yet never dared wish for. After his father's death his mother had broken inside. She'd been completely rudderless without Ilya's dad and, once she'd worked through the initial stages of her grief, she'd changed on a level that left Ilya confused and worried for her—both her sanity and her safety. She'd thrown herself into dating just about any man who showed an interest in her, once admitting to doing so because she had to find a way to light the darkness that losing her husband had left inside her.

He'd seen his mom go from a loving wife, a doting mother, to a brittle, insecure woman. Not being able to fill the gaps of what was missing in her had been torture for him. When she and her current boyfriend had been killed in a reckless driving maneuver on the 101, no one had been surprised. Devastated, yes, but not surprised. And for Ilya, it had been a horrible awakening. He hadn't been able to save his father and he hadn't been able to save his mother, either. He was under no illusion that his need to control the world around him stemmed from that year of sheer hell, which made this normality all the sweeter. Or would, if he could think of a way to tell Yasmin about his involvement in her past. That night had been a defining moment in her life—would she ever be able to not think of that experience every time she looked at him once she learned the truth?

As they were cleaning up together after their meal he heard Yasmin's phone buzz on the counter.

"You gonna get that?" he asked, rinsing dishes and loading the dishwasher.

"Later."

"Might be important."

"It's not a number I recognize. If it's important they'll call again."

The phone stopped its vibration, then almost immediately started again.

"I'd better get that, then," Yasmin said with a wry look on her face.

He watched her. She looked a little scared to answer the call. Maybe not scared, exactly, but apprehensive. She walked out onto the patio and after what sounded like some stilted pleasantries, he heard the tone of her voice change and become quite animated. She came back into the kitchen after a few minutes with a cautious smile on her face.

"This is awkward. I have a potential new client who wants to meet my husband and we've been asked out to dinner. I totally understand if you decline, given our agreement not to discuss our businesses in our marriage."

"It was your stipulation," Ilya pointed out carefully.

"Which you didn't argue."

"True. If I had, the wedding wouldn't have gone ahead, right?"

She had the grace to look embarrassed. "Right," she answered tightly. "Look, forget it. I—"

"Yasmin, relax. It's a dinner. I think we can waive our rules this one time. It's obviously important to you or you wouldn't be asking me. When is it?"

"Tomorrow night?"

"Sure," he said, wiping his hands dry on a towel. "We can do that."

He saw her shoulders sag in relief. "Thanks. Um, you weren't competing for the Hardacre contract, too, were you?"

He shook his head. Horvath Aviation had considered it when the job went out for bids, but he had heard rumors about the guy and he didn't want to put any of his staff on the firing line should Wallace Hardacre make the type of inappropriate advance he was rumored to make. Yasmin obviously had put in a bid for the Hardacre contract, however, and he didn't quite know how that made him feel.

Immediately his protective instincts surged to the fore, and he wanted to warn her about what Hardacre could be like. But then an insidious thought wormed through from the back of his mind. Somewhere he'd heard about a deal Hardacre had made with his long-suffering wife, Esme—that he would never touch a married woman.

Was that why Yasmin had suddenly put her single status in the hands of Match Made in Marriage? Had she married solely to secure a business contract? And if she had, where did that leave him if she won it—or didn't? He was developing feelings for her that he hadn't expected. But was she using him? Had he, through no fault of his own, simply repeated the mistakes he'd made in his early twenties?

Oblivious to the turmoil racing around in his mind, Yasmin made them each a mug of decaf coffee. She looked happy. Genuinely happy and completely relaxed. He hated that he had to question it and wonder whether it was because she was with him or because she was on the cusp of reaching some business goal. Suddenly her insistence that they never discuss business took on a whole new meaning. And he didn't like it one little bit. But if she had her secrets, didn't he also? And until he was able to bare his truth to her, how could he demand the same of her?

Yasmin could barely contain her excitement as she got ready for bed. The dinner with Esme and Wallace Hardacre had gone extremely well and she felt certain that Carter Air was the Hardacres' preferred carrier.

She'd had a moment of discomfiture yesterday when she'd wondered if Horvath had bid for the Hardacre contract, as well, but Ilya's assurance they hadn't lifted her heart and her hopes for Carter Air. Maybe now they'd have the stability they so desperately needed. She wouldn't need to let any of her respected team go and she'd be able to pay her loan back in full. And the icing on the cake was the burgeoning relationship she had with Ilya.

The only fly in the ointment right now was those emails. Another one had come through while they'd been at dinner.

You're not listening to me. Leave him now or everyone will know what you're really like.

She'd seriously thought about blocking *hisgirl* but caution had stayed her hand. So far the emails had been empty threats—more nuisance than anything. Certainly nothing she felt she could take to the police. And did she want the police involved, anyway? One thing was certain: she couldn't possibly comply with the demands. And even if she did what she was being told and left Ilya, what would that achieve for *hisgirl*? Was she standing in the wings, waiting to swoop in and take Yasmin's place in his life? She shook her head at her reflection in the mirror. She had to hope it would all just die a natural death if she continued to ignore the messages.

Ilya was already in bed when she finished in the bathroom. She snuggled up to his back and put one arm around his waist.

"Tired?" she asked, her fingers stroking his bare belly.

"Yeah," he answered.

His fingers closed around hers, halting her slow

but inexorable movement down his stomach. She accepted the rejection without taking it to heart. Since that first night they'd made love, sleep had been low on their agenda when they'd gone to bed.

"Tonight went well, don't you think?" she said softly against his back.

He grunted an assent. He really must be exhausted, she thought.

"Ilya?"

"Hmm?"

"Were you…?"

She struggled to find the right words, and when she fell silent Ilya sighed and rolled over to face her.

"Was I what?" he prompted.

"Were you going out with anyone before we got married? Anyone you were serious about?"

"No."

His answer was short and emphatic.

"Oh."

"Why do you ask?"

"No reason. Goodnight."

He rolled back onto his side. "G'night."

She lay in the darkened room and listened to his steady breathing. She was almost sure he wasn't asleep. Something was bugging him, but what? When she thought about it, she realized he'd changed after she mentioned the Hardacres last night. In fact, last night had been the first night they hadn't made love since their first time together. She'd put that down to the fact they'd sated themselves with each other at her apartment but maybe there was something else.

Had he been lying to her when he'd said Horvath Aviation hadn't bid for the contract? No, surely not. It would have come out in the conversation at the dinner table tonight. Instead, Esme had talked about their wedding and the joy of being newlyweds, as if reinforcing to her husband that Yasmin was completely out of bounds. Wallace had been happy to discuss golf and the latest ball game results with Ilya. In fact, the conversation had been completely social—not touching on business at all.

So what had gotten under his skin? She wanted to know. Wanted to make it better for him. After yesterday and opening up to him about her college hazing, he'd been so loving, so gentle. And fierce, too, when he'd told her that none of it was her fault. She'd believed him, not only because she'd wanted to, but because she trusted him.

Trust was a fragile thing. Like spun glass. In the wrong hands it could be shattered into a thousand painful shards. But in the right ones, it could be treasured and loved. Was that what she was learning to feel for her husband? Love? She had nothing to compare the feeling with, but the way both her mind and her body reacted when she was with Ilya seemed to indicate that she was very definitely falling for him. It was more than she'd hoped for. More than she'd ever thought she deserved. And all because of him.

She shifted in the bed, trying to get a bit more comfortable, but it felt strange now to try to fall asleep without her limbs entwined with her husband's.

She found herself thinking about her grandfather.

He most definitely would have disapproved of this union, but he wasn't here anymore. He'd been her guide growing up, but at her darkest moment she hadn't been able to turn to him for support. She'd struggled through the worst time of her life on her own and had come through on the other end stronger and more determined to succeed without the help of anyone else. But sometimes, she acknowledged, she couldn't do it all on her own.

She considered Jim Carter's bitterness toward the Horvaths purely because he'd been the jilted lover. Alice had broken his heart and he'd built a lifetime of resentment over the fact, poisoning Yasmin's mind about the other private aviation company and its owners from the day her parents had parked her on his doorstep. But Ilya was nothing like the type of man her granddad had told her he was.

You barely know him and you think you're in love with him? She didn't know if the voice in her mind was her own or an echo of her grandfather's, and as it played in her thoughts she couldn't sleep. Something had shifted between her and Ilya. Something she couldn't put her finger on. Something wasn't right.

Twelve

It felt odd to drive toward work together, especially with this awkward new invisible wall that had appeared between them over the weekend. They'd left Ilya's Lamborghini in the garage, taking his brand-new Tesla, instead.

Ilya dropped Yasmin at the front door of Carter Air. He hadn't rebuffed her attempt to kiss him as she'd gotten out the car, but he hadn't exactly turned it into a fond farewell, either. Maybe it was because of the puppy, she thought, as she snapped a leash on his collar and undid his puppy seat belt harness to get him out of the car. Blaze had shown an unholy interest in the armrest next to him and the leather upholstery now bore a less-than-charming set of tooth marks. Ilya had not looked impressed when he'd seen the damage.

Or maybe Ilya was just worried about something waiting for him at Horvath Aviation and had switched into work mode already. She let the puppy go to the bathroom before taking him into the office building attached to Carter Air's main hangar.

The moment Yasmin set foot inside, Riya shot out of her chair to envelope Yasmin in a massive hug.

"Welcome back!" the petite office manager gushed before stepping back to appraise her boss. "Well, well, well, marriage obviously suits you. Look at that glow!"

Yasmin felt her face suffuse with color. "It's just a tan. I laid around the pool a lot."

"Oh, sure, I believe you," Riya answered with a giggle.

"It's true," Yasmin protested, then couldn't help but join in her friend's laughter. She looked around the office. "So, what's new? What do I need to attend to first?"

The two women went into Yasmin's office. Blaze flopped down in a corner and dozed off. Yasmin had taken him for a long walk earlier this morning, to burn off some of his energy so she'd be able to concentrate on work for a few hours, at least. Hannah had suggested leaving him at the house but she wanted to get the puppy used to a varied routine, which included having him learn how to behave at work with either her or Ilya.

"This courier delivery arrived just before you did,"

Riya said with a massive grin and handed over a legal envelope to her boss.

Yasmin felt her heartbeat speed up. She recognized the name of the attorneys printed in the corner of the envelope. They acted for the Hardacres. She took a deep breath, opened the flap and shook the contents onto her desk. And there it was, the signed contract in black and white. Joy and relief competed for equal space inside her.

"We did it," she said triumphantly, looking up at Riya with a big grin. "We got the contract."

"That's great news. I never doubted you for a minute. They'd have been crazy to accept anyone else's offer. What a great way to kick off the week. I'll let the team know. When do we start with them?"

"Friday," Yasmin said scanning the letter that accompanied the contract. The *signed* contract, she thought with an inner shimmer of happiness. "They have a family trip to Palm Springs."

"It's a good thing we can fit them in, then, isn't it?" Riya said with a wink as she headed out to the main office.

Bookings had been well down these past few months and the relief Yasmin felt was huge. She took her time to read through the contract again, her eyes lingering on the morality clause. Esme Hardacre had insisted upon it, partly to keep her husband's wandering hands in check but also to act as a warning to anyone who looked at the charismatic motivational coach and speaker as fair game. Yasmin hadn't balked at it when she'd bid for the business and had read the initial contract draft as part of the tender process. But now? Given the weird emails she was getting?

She pushed her concerns about the morality clause aside as something that would not be a concern. She'd met Esme's strict criteria and she would continue to do so. That's all there was to it.

Blaze sat up and barked, his nap quite clearly over.

"Wanna go and meet the team?" she said to the little guy, clipping his leash back on. "C'mon, they're going to love you."

As the days went by, getting back into a routine workweek was both satisfying and a little frustrating. Yasmin found herself missing Ilya at odd moments during the day. Even Riya had caught her wistfully staring out her office window toward Horvath Aviation. All the staff had been thrilled about the new contract, approaching their work with renewed vigor and enthusiasm. Yasmin realized the problem hadn't just been hers to bear alone and it was good to know that they were going to be okay. Now, if only she could get to the bottom of why Ilya had become withdrawn in the past few days.

Yasmin had started to use her own truck to get to and from work. It was much older than anything in Ilya's fleet and more dog-friendly. He hadn't argued when she'd suggested she transport Blaze in the old Ford, but also hadn't suggested he accompany them in it, either. The last two nights, Ilya had worked late into the night, sliding into bed after she'd finally given in and fallen asleep. The honeymoon was very definitely over.

* * *

Ilya arrived at his grandmother's on Thursday morning. As he got out of the Tesla, his eye caught on the damage wrought by Blaze, and he made yet another mental note to book an appointment to get it repaired.

He straightened his suit and walked toward the imposing front door of the house his grandfather had ordered built for his bride when he'd made his first million dollars. Old Eduard's love for Alice showed in every line and curlicue of the building; it represented nothing less than a small Hungarian palace. It should have looked incongruous here in California, but with the landscaping and plantings that had been done, it fit into the surroundings as if it had been there for centuries.

The front doors swung open and Alice stood there waiting for him.

"Nagy," he murmured, leaning down to kiss her crepe-soft cheek.

A whisper of her fragrance swirled around him, the floral, powdery scent one he always associated with her, no matter who he encountered wearing it.

"My boy," she patted his cheek. "What brings you here today?"

"We need to talk."

Her smile faded and a serious look crept into her eyes. "Well, then. You'd better come through to my sitting room. Can I offer you anything to eat or drink?"

"This isn't really a social call."

She sniffed in response and straightened her already ramrod-stiff posture even further before leading the way to her private sitting room. Ilya preferred it to the larger room she used when she entertained the extended family or large groups of friends. This room was more intimate and definitely more her.

"What is it?" she demanded.

Alice was nothing if not direct, and Ilya had inherited that from her. But now that he was here, the words that hovered on the edge of his tongue sounded churlish. He knew his grandmother took her matches very seriously. Questioning her about Yasmin was questioning Alice's integrity at the same time. But his grandmother also had a great respect for honesty so he decided to come straight out and ask her the question that had been plaguing him since the dinner with the Hardacres.

"Did Yasmin marry me to secure her new client?"

His grandmother blinked at him. "I beg your pardon?"

Ilya quickly explained the situation with the Hardacres. To her credit, Alice didn't immediately shoot him down for being an idiot. Instead, she sat back in her armchair and studied him carefully.

"And how does that make you feel? To think she might have used you?"

He gave her a sharp look. "Angry, exploited."

"Have you asked her about it?"

"Of course not."

"You're husband and wife, aren't you? Shouldn't

you bring your concerns to each other before you seek outside counsel?"

He snorted. "Nagy, you're hardly outside counsel."

"That's true," she acknowledged with a small smile. "But if your marriage is to work, and your reaction to your suspicions makes me believe that you're already well invested in this coupling, you need to learn to work through issues like this together."

She was right, and it irritated the hell out of him to have to admit it. It didn't stop him asking his next question, though.

"You investigated her, didn't you?"

"As my people investigated you also. You agreed to that, if you remember, and it's a prerequisite for being accepted as a client with Match Made in Marriage. No exceptions."

He waved his hand in acknowledgement but then he froze and looked her directly in the eyes. "Just how far back did your investigation go, Nagy?"

Alice's lips formed a straight line. "As far as was necessary, my boy."

"You know about her hazing, don't you," he said with sudden clarity.

The barest inclination of her head gave him the answer he sought.

"How long?" he demanded through clenched teeth.

"Since you finally saw Jennifer Morton for the person she truly is. You hardly think I wouldn't have made discreet inquiries into what led you to break your engagement, do you? You arrived home a broken man. I had to know why."

She'd seen him at his worst—not once, not twice, but three times as he'd lost the three people in his life he'd thought were most important to him. Those losses, the scars they'd left deep inside him, had held him back. And, as much as he hated the reminder, when it came to Yasmin he was still holding back.

Alice drew in a breath, and he saw her fingers tremble slightly as she began to speak again. "Ilya, the only way for a relationship to thrive is with love and honesty. I believe the two of you are likely on the path to love. You both need to work on honesty. I cannot tell you anything that you can't find out for yourself simply by speaking to your wife. Settle this between you. Don't let your pride, or what happened with Jennifer, ruin what could be the best thing to happen to both you and Yasmin."

"But what about her reasons—?"

Alice put up a hand to stop him. "No buts. You each had your reasons for entering your marriage. What you do with it is now up to you. You didn't expect to find love, and I imagine that Yasmin didn't either, but you belong together, I cannot stress that enough. Work this out, Ilya. *Talk* to your wife."

She rose from her seat and Ilya did also, knowing he was being dismissed.

As Ilya drove back home, his mind was whirling. Nothing Nagy did should surprise him and yet today she'd trumped everything with her revelation. Her conviction that he and Yasmin belonged together was unshakeable. And he had to admit yet again, on the face of things, everything appeared to support that conviction. The time he and Yasmin had spent together so far had underlined their deep compatibility on so many levels. So why did it bother him so much that Yasmin might have used their marriage to leverage her chance to win the Hardacre contract? As his grandmother had so rightly pointed out, he'd entered into their match with his own agenda of companionship and children. He'd never expected love…

He wasn't being entirely fair to Yasmin. Carter Air had to be struggling. It was a tough industry and, up until his death, Jim Carter had been holding on by the threads that bound his overalls. Ilya knew Yasmin was proud and stubborn and determined. They were characteristics he was intimately acquainted with himself. Would he have turned to marriage as a solution if their business circumstances were reversed? If he was totally honest with himself, he knew he'd do whatever it took, which was exactly what Yasmin had done.

All that self-talk about commitment had been a crock. At the first hurdle, he'd fallen. He needed to do better and make it up to her. Nagy had impressed honesty upon him. That meant he had to quit putting off telling Yasmin about his part in her hazing. He had to open up the lines of communication between them and approach her about this like a reasonable and rational human being and, if not entirely rational, then like a husband who had truly begun to care for his wife.

Thirteen

Yasmin looked up from her flight plan for the next day as a message notification pinged on her laptop screen. She opened her email program. One unread message. Her skin crawled when she saw who it was from—*hisgirl*. There'd been nothing since the night of the dinner with the Hardacres and Yasmin had been hoping that the person had given up. Apparently not.

Her eyes scanned the subject header: I warned you.

She clicked on the message but there was no content. Nothing. Just that header. What the heck did that mean? They'd warned her. So what?

The phone on her desk started to ring, dragging her attention away from the computer.

"It's Esme Hardacre for you," her receptionist informed her before switching the call through.

"Esme, how lovely to hear from you. I'm just finalizing the flight plan for tomo—"

"You can forget it. In fact, you can forget everything. We're canceling our contract with you." The woman's voice was cold and hard, as if every word spoken was carved from ice.

"What? Why?" Yasmin blurted out.

"I thought you were better than that. Was my husband to be the next feather in your cap? Seriously, you need help."

"Esme, please. Can you explain?"

But she was talking to dead air. Yasmin quickly punched in the number for Hardacre Industries, her fingers trembling. What the heck had just happened?

"This is Mrs. Hardacre's assistant," came a disembodied voice in her ear when she identified herself and asked to be put through to Esme.

"I need to speak with Mrs. Hardacre, please."

"Mrs. Hardacre is not taking calls."

"Look, she just called me. I really need to talk to her. I'd like some explanation."

"Explanation?" the tone of the man's voice just about shriveled her ear. "The photos were bad enough but I think the video is all the explanation the Hardacres needed."

"What video?" Yasmin demanded, but she felt an icy finger of inevitability drag through her. Was this what *hisgirl* had meant about being warned?

"I just sent you an email," came the assistant's succinct reply before the call was abruptly disconnected.

On cue, her computer pinged again. Yasmin shifted

her mouse, the cursor on the screen hovering over the new message. It had been forwarded, and she immediately saw that the original message was from her nemesis. As usual, it was succinct.

Be careful who you trust. Yasmin Carter is not as squeaky clean as she seems.

There were four attachments. Three photo files and one movie file.

Yasmin swallowed against the bile that rose in her throat as she opened the first photo. Her blood ran cold as she recognized it immediately as the one sent to her two weeks ago. She flicked through to the next photo and the next, feeling sicker with each one, but the video was by far the worst. It had been taken just before she had her last vodka shot and entered the water for her final challenge.

While so much of that night remained a blur, parts of it she could recall. They'd blindfolded her and spun her around. She'd dropped to her knees. She could still remember the sensation of the gritty sand embedding in her skin, remembered the vertigo and the nausea that had assailed her. In the video she'd been told to strip down to her underwear, to the shouts and catcalls of the young women surrounding her. She'd tried to stand, she remembered that, and lost her balance, sprawling on her back in the sand. A sex toy had landed on the ground next to her and a disembodied voice could be heard coaxing her to use it or forfeit.

Yasmin closed the window before she saw the rest.

Her stomach heaved and she shot to her feet and raced for the bathroom. Riya looked up from her desk as Yasmin ran down the hall.

"Yasmin? Are you okay?"

She couldn't speak. She made it to the bathroom just in time, only just managing to lock the door behind her before her stomach erupted. Even though she couldn't remember all the details of that night, it had been her worst nightmare. It had been something she'd done her best to get over, to forget, to rise above. And now it had been broadcast to her client. Whoever was behind this must hate her very much. Sending those files to the Hardacres was vindictive and cruel. And it had lost her everything.

Her stomach heaved again, but there was nothing left. How symbolic, she thought bitterly. There really was nothing left.

What on earth was *hisgirl*'s agenda? And how on earth was she going to hold her company together, let alone repay her loan? She had to take this to the police now. The damage that had been wrought by *hisgirl* was criminal, surely. But the thought of showing the files to the police, of reliving it all again and again had her dry retching once more.

"Yasmin?" Riya was at the door, gently knocking.

"I'm okay," Yasmin croaked. "Be out in a minute."

She hauled herself up to her feet and flushed the toilet, then went to the basin, rinsed her mouth and splashed her face with cold water. She eyed her reflection in the mirror. A pale face with stricken eyes stared back at her—her features a far cry from those of the girl in the video. But they were one and the same person and, it seemed, tarred with the same brush.

Ilya had said what had happened to her that night hadn't been her fault but she knew how others would see it because she saw it that way herself. She could have walked away before it got to the point where she was no longer able to make decisions for herself. She could have called a halt to the increasingly degrading activities the queen bee of the sorority demanded of her.

Yes, she understood that others were also to blame, that essentially she'd been in their care, but deep down inside she still felt *she* was ultimately the one who'd made the choice to sacrifice her dignity just to fit in. And with what she'd chosen to do that night, she'd sacrificed everything her grandfather had worked so hard to build—everything she herself had worked so hard to hold on to. She'd failed. Again.

Riya was still on the other side of the door when Yasmin came out of the bathroom.

"Something I ate," she said in explanation as she brushed off Riya's concern and moved past her friend to head back to her office.

Changing her mind partway there, she went through the door that led to the hangar. She stood in the high-ceilinged building that her grandfather had built from the ground up nearly seventy years ago. The building that had consumed him, that had been his sole source of satisfaction his whole working life. The building she'd put up as security for her wedding loan. She looked at the Beechcraft she'd added to the small fleet, at the mechanics doing the final check for the flight plan that would no longer be executed tomorrow.

That would be the first plane she'd have to let go. She'd opted to buy rather than lease—a business tenet she'd inherited from her grandfather. It had left Carter Air with no financial buffers. She loved flying the twin, but without the demand for it, she'd have to sell it—and hopefully for enough to cover the short-term loan she'd taken out to get married.

She wandered through the hangar, feeling as though her heart was breaking, and let her eyes drift over the smaller craft. There was a chance she might be able to pass them to the flying school that operated out of the airfield and recover something of her losses there if she was lucky. Despair and helplessness threatened to drive her to her knees. Bit by bit her fleet and her team would have to go. She had no avenues left open to her anymore. She drifted into her private hangar next door, to her Ryan. It would have to go, too. Her plane, the hangar, her apartment. She couldn't afford to hold on to any of it if Carter Air crumbled. She was numb with grief and all the while questions kept echoing in her head. Why? Who? What next?

She breathed in the air redolent with fuel. A smell that was as much a part of her as her DNA. Maybe she'd get a job working for someone else, but would her staff? They were her responsibility and she'd let them down.

Yasmin sensed a movement behind her, caught a familiar hint of pine and sandalwood. Ilya. She turned to face him.

"Riya called me. She said you weren't well."

"She didn't need to do that. As you can see, I'm quite fine."

He looked at her. Really looked, and she felt as if he was probing beneath the surface, seeing the rot that lay beneath.

"You don't look fine. Maybe you should let me take you home."

"Really, I'm okay. Besides, I have to pick up Blaze from puppy day care," she hedged.

She couldn't go home yet. Not when she had to explain to her team that things had taken a turn for the worse. That there was no Hardacre contract anymore. Ilya reached out one finger, touched her cheek and then held his finger, moist from the tears she hadn't even realized she was crying, up for her perusal.

"That doesn't say fine to me."

She closed her eyes for a moment, her hands forming tight fists at her sides. Then she forced herself to open her eyes. She had to tell someone about losing the Hardacre business. She might as well start with him.

"The Hardacres changed their minds. They no longer wish to use Carter Air as their carrier."

"What? They can't do that. You have a contract."

She swallowed and looked away for a moment. "Had a contract. There was a morality clause that they insisted on, that I agreed to."

"Okay, but I still don't see why they ditched you."

Yasmin dragged in a breath. "Do you remember what I told you about my hazing?"

He nodded, his face taking on a serious cast that gave her a glimpse into the hard-nosed businessman she'd always understood him to be.

"I don't see what that has to do with anything."

"It seems that conduct unbecoming has no expiry date. Someone sent them photos and video of that night. As a result, they no longer require my services."

Ilya couldn't believe the words that came from Yasmin's mouth. No wonder she looked so haggard. He reached for Yasmin, pulled her to him. She came willingly, her slender form fitting against him, her arms sliding around his waist. The front of his shirt grew damp with her tears and he felt his heart shatter with the knowledge that she was in so much pain.

He'd planned to tell Yasmin everything tonight. To lay his own misjudgment of Jen's character and his involvement with Yasmin's hazing on the table and beg her forgiveness for both not telling her sooner and for not reporting Jen long ago. But with Yasmin as shell-shocked and vulnerable as she was, how could he throw that in her face now?

The way he saw it, there was only one person who could be attacking Yasmin and that was his ex-fiancée. If he'd acted earlier none of this would be happening now. But one thing was for sure. It stopped now. He'd track Jen down and he'd make sure she faced the full consequences of her actions. But first he had to make things right for his wife.

"We'll work something out," he said firmly.

"There's nothing left to work out. I'm going to have to wind up. Not immediately, but over the next couple of months. We're barely making enough to cover fuel and wages as it is."

He'd had no idea that things were so bad.

"We'll find a way, Yasmin, I promise."

"You can't promise something you have no control over!" she retorted, pushing herself away from him.

Ilya reached for her hand, determined to keep a connection with her. To try and infuse in her some level of trust that together they could sort this out.

"Let's go into your office. We can talk better there and you can show me Carter Air's current financials. There must be something we can do."

Several hours later Ilya pushed back from Yasmin's computer and rubbed at the tension in his neck. It was a miracle Yasmin had held onto Carter Air this long. He'd suspected the company had been in a bad position long before she'd taken over and he'd speculated that the only way she'd survived was by shaving costs dramatically to be able to undercut her competition on contract bids, but he'd had no idea by how much.

She'd barely been drawing a salary. Probably only enough to cover her utilities, food and fuel for her truck and the Ryan. But she hadn't stinted on costs where it mattered most: staff and maintenance. And then there was the loan she'd admitted to taking out to go ahead with the wedding. He sighed in frustration. He could see why she'd done it but she'd had no safety net in case things fell through. And they had fallen through.

There was a way forward, but only if she'd put her pride and fierce independence aside. Would she go for it?

For a brief moment, he wondered where she'd be right now if Carter Air had closed before she'd taken it over, if her grandfather had let go of his own inability to admit defeat when the writing had been on the wall for more years than Ilya cared to think about. It seemed so grossly unfair that Jim Carter had pushed the yoke of expectation onto his granddaughter. What would she have wanted to do if this hadn't been the expectation thrust upon her most of her adult life? And what kind of a husband was he, that he hadn't even asked her that simple question?

"It's bad, isn't it?" Yasmin said.

"Yeah, I can't sugarcoat it, Yasmin. You've done a great job keeping things going so far, but as you pinpointed a while back, you need a long-term, steady flow of income to push you over the hump and into a more viable position."

"And I don't have that anymore."

"Are you sure you're not willing to discuss it further with the Hardacres?"

She vehemently shook her head. "I tried. They won't even take my calls. As far as they're concerned I'm in breach of contract and, Ilya, to be honest, I don't want this to blow up any further than it already has."

"And you're not prepared to let me have my legal team look at it?" Maybe if he got his people onto this they might be able to confirm his suspicions about who was responsible for sending the photos and video. But Yasmin was adamant.

"Absolutely not."

"Then there's only one thing left."

"Declare bankruptcy."

"No, not yet, anyway. I have some ideas that might allow you to continue operations and get you on your feet. But you're not going to like them."

Yasmin chewed on her lower lip. "You're not going to offer to buy me out, are you?"

"That is an option. Do you want me to?"

"No. I'd rather close tomorrow than do that."

Ilya took the blow like a punch to the gut. "That makes your feelings pretty clear."

"I'm sorry. I just couldn't. You don't understand. My grandfather—"

"Your grandfather let his pride and bitterness get in the way of far too much. Are you going to do the same?" he demanded, too frustrated with himself to realize he was beginning to lose patience with his beautiful but stubborn bride. "He's dead, Yasmin. And you're not. You're facing some serious financial issues here—it's not just you, it's your whole staff and the clients you currently have who will be affected—and yet you're just as stubborn as the old man was. You need help."

She blinked and looked away. *Oh, hell, no.* Not tears again. His mother's tears had always been his undoing and he'd never felt so helpless in his life as when he faced a crying woman—especially one he had feelings for. He hated that he had to be so blunt, but there was nothing else left to do. He watched Yasmin as she pulled herself together and turned back to face him.

"What's your suggestion?" She enunciated carefully, as if every word had to be pulled from her.

"That Horvath Aviation assign our smaller contract work to you." He held up a hand as she started to interrupt. "No, hear me out. It's not a pity offer. It's purely a business decision we've been batting around in the boardroom for a while already. We considered branching out with another arm of Horvath Aviation that concentrated solely on the kind of work you do. As you know, it's a fiercely competitive niche and after completing our studies, we decided it wasn't viable for us to pursue it with our existing fleet. So this is what I suggest."

Ilya spent the next half hour outlining how he thought they could handle it.

"And, in doing this, I want to make you a personal loan to cover the money you borrowed for the wedding."

"No!" She shot out of her seat.

Ilya looked at her and willed her to understand where he was coming from with his offer. He had to make this right, even if he couldn't explain the full reasons why right here and now. Guilt plucked at him.

If only he hadn't allowed Jen to persuade him not to report the hazing for what it really was. If only he could turn back time. Was this what Nagy had expected of him? That he'd finally repair the damage done to Yasmin more than ten years ago? Well, he accepted that challenge. Right here, right now. He put every ounce of persuasion he could into his voice as he continued. "It's a personal loan, Yasmin. Between you and me. No one else needs to know about it. You can make payments to me when you're drawing a regular salary again, which I'd advise you commence as soon as we've ironed out the finer points of the subcontracting deal. Either that, or you're going to have to allow me to invest in Carter Air—either personally or through Horvath Aviation.

"You can see the writing on the wall as well as I can, Yasmin. Without an injection of money somewhere, you have no choice but to close. You won't be able to meet your loan repayments, you won't be able to meet fuel costs, wages, insurance. It's your choice. Are you going to insist on standing on your pride, or will you accept a hand offered in a genuine expression of help?"

Fourteen

None of what he'd said came as a surprise, and yet there was a part of her that still wanted to argue she could do this on her own. Sell a few planes, downsize and then just possibly be able to hang on by her fingernails for just a bit longer. But at the same time, she couldn't let down the staff that relied on her to make the kind of sound decisions that would keep them in stable employment. And what would she be left hanging on to? A skeleton of what Carter Air had been?

She felt sick to her stomach. She knew she had to accept Ilya's offer of assistance—at the very least accept the subcontracting offer. It would be a start, even though it left her beholden to both him and his company's largesse. A month ago she would never have considered this as an option, but right now, it was the only thing standing between her and bankruptcy. Yasmin forced herself to calm down and settle herself back in her seat. She pressed her hands down on the tops of her thighs to try and stop them shaking.

"Okay."

She had to do whatever it took to make it all right. And *hisgirl* needed to be stopped before they did anything else. Maybe if she'd taken the earlier emails to the police this wouldn't have happened. As soon as she'd ironed things out with Ilya, she was going to the police.

"Okay?" Ilya repeated.

"Yes, I agree to Carter Air subcontracting work to Horvath Aviation and I accept your offer of a personal loan to repay the bank for the money I borrowed for the wedding."

Even as she said the words she felt the weight of sole responsibility begin to lift from her shoulders. The sensation was such a release. She'd been so adamant about not involving Ilya in Carter Air in any way, but his insights proved invaluable. And there'd been no blame or recrimination from him, either. Just solid strength and support. Was this what a real marriage felt like? The knowledge that someone always had your back, without judgment or recriminations, no matter what?

Ilya heaved a huge sigh and smiled. "We'll work it out, you'll see. Would you also consider agreeing to my financial people taking a look at the long-term situation for Carter Air?"

Yasmin looked at him in surprise. In the back of her mind she could hear her grandfather's howl of outrage that she could even consider relinquishing so much control to a Horvath. But, from what she'd seen in the past few weeks, Jim Carter had been wrong about Ilya and his family. All they'd done was be helpful. She firmly pushed the embedded suspicions aside.

"Yasmin?"

"Fine, do what you have to, but I insist on being involved every step of the way. No decisions will be made without my okay."

"And what about the information that went to the Hardacres? Will you let me look into that?"

"No. Absolutely not. I will handle it," she said unequivocally.

Ilya reached across the desk and wrapped his fingers around her clenched fist.

"I know this isn't easy for you, Yasmin. I'll make sure my people keep you in the loop. Now," he said, rising from his seat, "shall we go home?"

She looked at the clock on the wall and realized, in horror, that she was supposed to have picked Blaze up from doggy day care by now.

"Oh, no, I'm running late!"

"I asked Hannah to collect Blaze for us when you went to get the files from Riya."

"You think of everything, don't you?"

"Control freak, remember?" he said.

His lips curved into a smile that, even through all the turmoil she was facing, managed to hit her square in the chest and spread warmth through her body. She laughed.

"How could I forget?" she answered drily as she gathered her things. "You're totally in your element."

"Let's ride home together," he suggested. "I can drop you off here in the morning."

She was about to protest but exhaustion pulled at every part of her. "Okay, thanks."

"What? No argument?"

"I'm bowing to your control freakiness, all right?"

He gave her another one of those smiles. "Yeah. And, Yasmin…" He paused reaching for her hand and threading his fingers with hers. "We've got this. Together we'll get you through."

I hope so, Yasmin thought to herself as they exited the building and got into Ilya's car to go home. All the way back to Ojai she remained silent, her mind churning with the day's events, how Ilya had strode in like some knight in shining armor and saved the day. Was that what their marriage was to be like? Her making mistakes, him coming along and solving her problems and making her depend on him more and more? It felt so unbalanced, so unlike her to rely so heavily on another person.

No, whichever way she looked at it she had no other choice than to accept Ilya's offer of help. She made the right decision for her company and her staff. But there was one thing she would do on her own—tomorrow she would contact the police.

* * *

Yasmin went to bed early that night but Ilya wasn't far behind. She felt the mattress dip slightly as he got under the covers. They hadn't made love for days and right now she wasn't sure if she even wanted to, but her body craved him. Craved being close to him. Craved that sense that no matter what was wrong, she was safe in his arms. When he reached for her she went willingly, curving her body against his and resting her head on his chest.

Beneath her ear his heart beat was strong, steady and true.

"You okay?" he asked in the dark, the rumble of his voice tickling her ear.

"I'll be fine. It's a lot to get my head around."

"You've made the right choice."

She nodded. She knew that. Sometimes the right choices weren't the easy ones, were they?

Ilya stroked the back of her head. "I've missed you."

"I wasn't the one who pulled away."

"I know. I'm sorry. I had some stuff to work out."

"And you couldn't discuss it with me?"

He huffed out a breath that could have been a laugh. "Seems we both have a lot to learn about being married and sharing, doesn't it?"

He was right, as much as she hated to admit it. He spoke again.

"Shall we agree that in the future, if you need anything, any kind of help, you'll come to me. In work and here, at home. I'm your husband. You need to tell me when something's wrong."

She stiffened, her extreme self-reliance protesting. But, she reminded herself, without Ilya's help and suggestions today, Carter Air would be facing a very different future.

"Okay, yes, I agree."

The words came from her reluctantly. Years of being her grandfather's sounding board and right hand had left their mark. You didn't just undo a lifetime of conditioning in one horrible day.

Ilya's arms squeezed her tight. "Thank you," he murmured against the top of her head. "We can make this work, if we work together."

Despite his reassurance, Yasmin realized he hadn't mentioned anything about coming to her if the need for support was reversed. Did he still expect to be there for her, while not needing her in return? Or maybe there was something else holding him back. Something she didn't know about. Maybe he had some other agenda behind his offer of help? She told herself to stop being so silly, to simply take his very generous offer at face value. But she wasn't Jim Carter's granddaughter for nothing, and even though Ilya had come through for her today in ways she'd never have anticipated, something felt off.

Ilya woke to the delicious heaviness of Yasmin still sprawled across him. He traced one finger down her back. Her skin instantly broke out in a trail of goose bumps following the path of his touch. She stretched against him and his body quickened the way it always did when she was around. His hand continued on its journey, his fingers tickling the base of her spine where her back curved in just so, then traveled lower to cup the curve of her bottom.

"Good morning to you, too," she murmured against his chest.

He rolled Yasmin onto her back and bent to nuzzle the side of her neck. "It's about to be a very good morning," he whispered in her ear.

His phone rang.

"Ignore it," she whispered in *his* ear.

Her hands moved swiftly to his body, skimming his shoulders, his chest, his belly. The phone continued to ring.

"I'm going to have to take it," he groaned in frustration and dragged himself away from her.

He grabbed his phone from the nightstand and, seeing it was the general manager of his East Coast subsidiary on the line, stabbed the screen with one finger to accept the call. It was hard for him to concentrate on the message being relayed to him as Yasmin sat up on the bed and whipped her nightgown off in one sleek movement. She tossed the garment at him and he caught her scent as he snatched the slip of silk from the air and let it slide through his fingers onto the bed. There was already a flush of arousal on her chest and her nipples were taut. He felt the deep throb of need pull through his body.

But suddenly the words "heart attack" and "hospital" caught his attention and he realized what was being said to him.

"I'll be there as soon as I can," he said, disconnecting the call.

Guilt and regret rippled through him at the thought of leaving Yasmin so soon after the turmoil of yesterday. Plus, as he'd finally drifted to sleep last night, he'd promised himself he would talk to her today about the secret he still withheld. Now he wouldn't have time to do either as his presence was urgently required in New York. He stopped her hands as they skimmed over him and dragged them to his lips, kissing her knuckles.

"I'm sorry. I'm going to have to take a rain check. Emergency at one of our subsidiaries."

Yasmin's demeanor changed in an instant. "Is it really serious?"

She slipped from the bed and pulled on a robe, tying the sash tight at her waist.

"Unfortunately, yes. The general manager of our East Coast office has had a massive heart attack. I need to go and fill in for him for a few days until we know what's happening."

"There's no one else you can send?"

He heard the silent plea in her voice and her vulnerability struck him to his core. If only it had been anyone other than Zachary Penney. He quickly explained to Yasmin. "This guy is a close friend of Nagy's. I owe it to his family, and mine, to be there."

"Of course. What can I do to help?"

She was instantly all business and he was infinitely grateful she was there. In no time she had him pushed in the direction of the bathroom while she packed a suitcase for him. By the time he was dressed and downstairs, she was already in the kitchen with a smoothie at the ready.

"You're going to regret not sharing your recipe with me," she said with a grin as she handed him the glass. "I had to guess."

He took a sip, grimaced, then downed the rest in one gulp. "You're right. It'll be first thing on my agenda when I get back."

"First thing?" Yasmin asked coyly, one fingertip tracing the outline of her nipple through the thin fabric of her robe.

He grinned. "Okay, second."

He leaned forward and gave her a hard kiss. "Thanks for everything. I'll call you tonight. And don't worry. I'll instruct the bank to make that transfer so you can settle your loan later today. Make sure you get the figures. My bank manager will be in touch."

"Don't worry about that now. It's not urgent."

"I'll deal with it."

Outside they could hear the beat of helicopter blades in the air.

"Sounds like your ride to the airport is here," Yasmin said, stepping close and hooking her arms around his neck. She pressed herself against his body and kissed him again. "Take care, huh?"

"You, too," he said.

In no time he was up at the helipad. He stowed

his case in the back of the chopper before taking the left-hand seat. When he took off, he circled over the house before heading to the airport. He usually relished tackling a challenge like this. Normally by now he'd be planning ahead as to how he could best ensure that the necessary contingencies were put in place quickly and efficiently. But this time, every cell in his body was attuned to the woman waving at him from below. He didn't just wish they'd been able to complete their morning together; he wished he didn't have to leave her, period.

He wasn't used to wanting someone like this. Sure, he had to make everything right for his family and loved them fiercely. But this was different. It left him daunted. After losing first his father, then his mother, and then being betrayed by his fiancée, he'd always believed that loving someone outside of his immediate family circle was inviting weakness, vulnerability. But he could no longer deny his growing feelings for Yasmin.

This was more than a crush, more than a lust-filled haze of need. Thinking she was using him to win the Hardacres' business had caused a knee-jerk reaction to pull away, as if he'd been looking for a reason for their marriage to fail, he could see that now. He was grateful to his grandmother for her guidance. He fought a smile. The older woman's knack for giving advice had been right on target. He did need to learn to open up, and so did Yasmin. As Nagy had so astutely pointed out, with honesty between them, they could do this.

Which brought him back to the secret he was holding back.

Would telling her destroy the fragile links they'd forged after yesterday? He had to tell her; it was a huge risk not to. The past had a way of coming back to a person and even though he hadn't been an instigator in the torment she'd endured, both back then and more recently, he had to act now to protect her as he ought to have done before.

He landed the helicopter at the airfield. A Gulfstream was waiting for him on the tarmac close by.

He wished he'd told her already. Of course, the right time to have done so would have been after she'd first disclosed to him who she was. But he couldn't turn back time. Nor could he turn around and go back to her right now. It would have to wait until he got home. He'd find a way to tell her everything because he hated having this secret lingering between them like a malignant stain on their relationship. And, despite Yasmin's refusal of his offer, he had every intention of discovering exactly who the Hardacre's informant had been so he would bring them to justice.

It was no longer enough to just be married. He realized now that he wanted it all. Everything that marriage to another human being entailed. Love, honor, respect, togetherness—right down to the very last wrinkle.

Fifteen

It had been four days—and four desperately lonely nights—since Ilya went away. For Yasmin, the days had been filled with walking and playing with the puppy, dealing with the contracts that had come across her desk from Horvath's legal team and flying the occasional client to their requested destination. But her nights were a different story. Sleep had become a fractured thing; she frequently paced the moonlit bedroom floor when wakefulness drove her from the bed.

Ilya had made a point of calling her each evening, and she found herself hanging onto the phone long after they'd said their goodbyes, reluctant to sever that ephemeral contact with him. A glance in the mirror this morning told her that pining for him was taking its toll, leaving dark shadows under her eyes. Ridiculous, when this coming weekend marked four weeks since they'd been married.

And what a roller coaster it had been so far, she thought as she settled Blaze in his crate for the night and wandered through to the office to fire up the computer. She had brought some work home with her and Ilya had told her to use the home computer if she ever needed it. On top of everything else going on, her laptop had died and she'd taken it in to get repaired.

She settled herself in the leather chair at the desk and sat for just a moment, closing her eyes and imagining him sitting here. She'd missed her parents when they'd gone traveling; she'd missed her grandfather when he'd passed away. But this felt different. It was a physical ache. She couldn't wait for Ilya to return home. Quick phone calls simply weren't enough.

How had he come to be such a vital part of her life so quickly? She'd always been the self-sufficient one, the solver of her own problems. The one others could rely on. It had often been a heavy responsibility to bear, but now it was as if Ilya had lifted that weight from her shoulders and bore it on his alone. Somehow they had to find a middle ground. She didn't want to give up every last bastion of control and independence, and she knew he didn't either, but she had growing confidence they could make it work.

He'd been as good as his word, and the money to repay her loan had appeared in her bank account the day he left for New York. Thankfully, there'd been no further fallout from the Hardacre debacle and she'd filed a complaint with the police, but Yasmin still walked around feeling as though there was yet another hammer blow still to drop. She hated feeling like this—as if turning the corner past that situation was just setting her up for another fall.

She spent about an hour checking through the Horvath subcontracting paperwork, making small notations here and there, before scanning the documents and emailing them to her lawyers for a final read through. Provided Ilya agreed to the minor tweaks she wanted, Carter Air had a future. She sat back in her chair for a moment and heaved a massive sigh of relief. She knew that good business generated more business. Working with the Horvaths might have been her grandfather's idea of hell on earth, but right now it was a godsend.

The deal with Horvath Aviation was ironclad. She knew Ilya would stand by his word because he was that kind of guy. This past month had taught her a lot about him. Not everything, obviously, and she looked forward to what she had yet to discover about her husband. Like, his most ticklish spots, she thought with a secretive smile. Or what movies he liked. She was a sucker for the old Bogie and Bacall black and whites herself. Maybe she'd organize a movie night for the two of them when he got back, and cook her special eggplant parmigiana.

She started mentally making a grocery list to give to Hannah as she logged into her mail before shutting down the computer. All thoughts of cooking and movie nights fled, however, when she saw the new message waiting in her inbox. Yasmin swallowed against the sick feeling that threatened to choke her as she opened it.

Your husband knows a lot more than he's telling you.

"What do you mean?" Yasmin all but shouted at the computer screen. "Enough with these stupid cryptic messages." Her fingers flew across the keyboard as she drafted a reply.

She kept it short and sweet.

You've done your worst. Now leave me alone.

She hit Send and went to close the window but a new message popped straight back up in her inbox.

You think that was my worst? He was at your hazing, did you know that?

"You're lying," Yasmin whispered in shock before keying those very words into the computer.

Again she hit Send but this time she waited for a reply. It didn't take long. Seconds later, email after email began to flood her inbox, each one with an attachment. Yasmin hesitated to open the first one but she figured that with Ilya's computer security being top-of-the-line she'd be safe. If the attachment had come with any viruses or malware, his software would block it.

The photo filled the screen and as she identified

the people in it, Yasmin's skin crawled in horror. It was a picture of Ilya—younger, certainly more carefree, but just as handsome as ever. But it wasn't Ilya who caused the visceral reaction that crawled through her body like some insidious vile disease. It was Jennifer Morton. The woman who'd strung her along, devised challenge after challenge for her, then almost killed her when Yasmin wouldn't back down. And she was tucked under Ilya's arm and looking up into his eyes, their smiles speaking volumes about their feelings for each other.

One by one, Yasmin trawled through the rest of the pictures. Her head was spinning by the time she got to the last one. It was a picture of a just-woken, sleep-mussed, naked Ilya in a bed. In the foreground was a photo of a woman's hand wearing an engagement ring. The picture was captioned, "I said yes!"

Another message came in. Feeling a sense of the inevitable, Yasmin opened it.

He was there that night. He knows how pathetic you are.

Ilya had been there?

Yasmin stayed frozen in her chair, staring at the screen. Emotions tumbled through her. Shock. Revulsion. Anger. But most of all, betrayal. Ilya knew it all. He'd seen her at her worst. He'd been party to her ultimate degradation. He'd been engaged to Jennifer Morton.

Why had he hidden the truth from her? She'd

opened her soul to him that day they'd gone up in the Ryan. Sure, she'd skirted a few of the more sordid details, but she'd bared virtually everything to him about what had happened and how it had affected her. Her eyes glazed over until she could no longer see the screen, but that didn't do anything to assuage the clawing pain that ripped inside her chest.

She'd trusted him with her greatest fear, and yet he'd known it all along. How could he have sat there, after they'd made love, and listened to her pouring her heart out and said nothing at all? Had this been some kind of joke to him? Was he, even now, laughing behind her back about how pitiful she'd been back then? How pitiful now? Was he somehow still in touch with Jennifer and were they laughing together? Or worse, was this all some elaborate scheme to wrest control of her business from her? Ilya had already said his firm had looked into branching out in the smaller client contracts market Carter Air flew, but that it hadn't been viable to establish a new division with that focus. But how much more viable would it be to take over an existing operation?

Yasmin could only be relieved that she'd refused to allow him to buy into Carter Air. Yes, she was still beholden to him for the personal loan, but her business, her life's blood, was still hers. Then there was the Horvath Aviation subcontract. But thinking about it now, it made her feel distinctly uncomfortable. How long had he been planning this? And was Jennifer involved? Were they in this together? Still quietly laughing at her behind her back? And what about Alice? Was she in on it, too? While every instinct urged her to email her lawyers immediately and tell them to instruct Horvath exactly where to shove its business, she couldn't do it to her staff. But no one said she had to stay here, or stay married to a man who'd withheld a vital truth from her.

She didn't sleep a wink that night. Instead, she spent all her time removing every last personal item she owned from the house and packing it into her truck. By the time Hannah arrived first thing in the morning, Yasmin was running on coffee and not a lot else.

"Are you okay, Mrs. Horvath?"

Yasmin barely managed not to roll her eyes. No matter how often she'd told Hannah to call her Yasmin or, if she must, Ms. Carter, she insisted on calling her Mrs. Horvath. Yasmin had begun not to notice so much, but this morning it succeeded in rubbing salt into an already exposed wound.

"Just a little tired is all," she answered, reaching for the coffee carafe and pulling a face when she realized it was empty. Again.

"Oh, you leave that to me. I'll make you a fresh pot," Hannah said, bustling past her and refilling the machine. "You must be missing Mr. Horvath, yes?"

Yasmin had been. She'd missed him as if a vital part of her was suddenly gone. Which, altogether, made her even more laughable, she realized. She closed her eyes a moment as they began to burn with more unshed tears and shook her head slightly.

All night she'd tried to understand why he hadn't

told her the truth about him and Jennifer. Would it have been so very hard? She was exhausted from wondering about his reasons, wondering what kind of man he really was, wondering why she'd allowed herself to fall in love with him. And that, she felt, was the biggest betrayal of all. He'd presented himself to her as the kind of man she'd only ever dreamed of meeting, but beneath it all, he was a fake.

She watched as Blaze walked outside on the patio, playing with a leaf that fluttered past before getting distracted by a chew toy that had been left under a sun lounger. Ilya had been so compassionate with the puppy. So determined to give him a home. Had that, too, been a lie constructed to somehow win her trust? For what purpose? None of it even made sense. All she knew is she needed to create some distance between them. She couldn't think here in his beautiful home because everything reminded her of him.

Blaze bounded in through the open patio doors and sat on her foot. She bent down and absently scratched his head and gave his chest a rub. What would she do with him? Was he even hers to take? He'd been found on Ilya's property, his care had been provided for by Ilya's cousin and paid for by Ilya himself. As much as it would break her heart, she had to leave Blaze behind.

Overhead, she heard the sound of a helicopter approaching the house. Her stomach tightened in a knot. Ilya had said nothing last night about coming home today. How on earth was she going to face him now, knowing what she did?

* * *

Ilya alighted from the chopper and gave Pete a thumbs-up after he'd taken his case from the back and walked clear of the helipad. He was exhausted but, as Valentin had wryly pointed out to him over a quick dinner together last night, what was he doing hanging around in New York when he had a beautiful wife waiting for him at home?

It had been a grueling few days away, but he was satisfied that not only was his general manager on the road to recovery, but everything else was in good hands for their operations to continue as normal. And, if old Zachary wasn't well enough in a few months to resume his duties, there was a succession plan in place so they could cross that bridge, too.

For now, though, all Ilya wanted was his wife. As busy as he'd been, he'd found his thoughts straying to her in unguarded moments and he'd missed her more than he would have thought possible. He'd kept his early arrival home a surprise, but given the fact he'd arrived by chopper, he figured she probably knew he was there by now. He felt strangely nervous, knowing what was coming—that he was about to reveal his part in her hazing and his desire to press historical charges—but not knowing how she would respond. He could only hope that the feelings they'd developed for one another would see them through.

It kind of surprised him that she hadn't come up to the helipad to welcome him home. Maybe she was out walking Blaze. If that was the case, he might have time to have a quick shower to erase the grime of travel before taking up again where they'd been interrupted before he'd had to fly East.

As he walked along the path, he heard the sound of Hannah's car going up the long driveway that led to the main road. It was strange that the housekeeper was heading out so early in the day when she normally would have only just arrived at the house. But it was nowhere near as strange as seeing Yasmin's truck parked in front of the house loaded with suitcases.

The front doors opened and the chill of foreboding that had begun to tickle at the back of his mind gave him a swift hard yank into reality when he saw the look on Yasmin's face.

"I wasn't expecting you," she said bluntly.

No welcome. No smile. No *Honey, I missed you.* Just a blank wall of…what? He wasn't sure exactly. All he knew was he needed to go into damage control mode.

"Hey," he answered her with a tentative smile. "I wanted to surprise you. Looks like I succeeded, huh?"

She gave him a bitter look in return. "Surprise. Yes, I guess you could call it that."

He swallowed. This wasn't going how he'd planned at all. When he left, he'd felt like they were on a pathway to a stronger future together. Even last night, when they'd spoken on the phone, hadn't there been affection and longing in her voice as they'd ended the call? What the hell had happened between then and now to change her into this cold effigy of the warm and caring woman he'd left only five mornings ago?

He drew nearer. "Where's Blaze?"

"Hannah took him to day care for me."

"I see."

Ilya didn't see at all. Why was Hannah taking the dog when the day care was on Yasmin's route to work? He looked at his wife's closed expression, trying to figure out what had changed between them since they spoke last night on the phone. He reached out to touch her.

"I missed you," he said, infusing his voice with all the longing that had been building since he left.

She neatly sidestepped his outstretched hand. "Please don't touch me."

Her words were delivered oh, so politely, but they felt like a vicious slap.

"Yasmin, what the he—?"

"You tell me what the hell," she demanded, her gray eyes dark and stormy. "Remember Jennifer Morton?"

If he'd walked straight into a propeller he couldn't have been more shocked. She knew. He'd left it too late.

"I can guess by the look on your face you do remember. How nice. But then again, it might have been nicer if you'd actually told me about it."

"That's not fair, Yasmin. We've barely begun to get to know each other. Jen, well, that was another time and place."

"Yes, exactly. A time and place that involved me, too, if you'll remember. A time and place I told you about when you asked me what my greatest fear was and yet, even despite my pouring my heart out to you about that night, you didn't think I deserved to know that you, my *husband*—" she spat the word as if it was a bitter, nasty taste in her mouth "—were there, too?"

"I can explain—" he started.

"I think it's gone beyond explanations, don't you? Have you any idea how betrayed I feel? I trusted you. And you were a part of that night all along. You and her!" She made a sound of disgust. "I should have kept on going when I left you at the altar. This whole charade, this fake marriage, was a disaster from the start. I can't help wondering why you even bothered to marry me. If all you wanted was to get your hands on my company then you could have just sat back and watched me go completely bankrupt and you could have picked up the bones of Carter Air for a song. You certainly didn't need to go to the bother of marrying me or having all those threatening emails sent to me.

"Which brings me to Jennifer—nice to know you two are still such great friends that she was prepared to help you. Exactly what is her stake in this? Were you planning to ditch me somewhere along the line, after your contemptible games with me, and renew your engagement with her?"

Her words came at him like machine-gun fire. They penetrated his mind but none of it made sense.

"We're over," she continued. "I will repay your loan as soon as possible. I will continue to subcontract to Horvath Aviation for as long as the offer remains. But I will not stay here as your wife."

She moved toward the driver's door of her truck but he beat her to it, pushing his weight against it so she couldn't open the door.

"What emails?"

Yasmin laughed. The sound was high-pitched, artificial.

"Out of everything I just said, that's what you focused on? Look, thanks for the memories, Ilya, and the sex. It was great while it lasted but I can't stay married to a man I cannot trust." She tugged her wedding ring off her finger and thrust it at him. "We're over."

Sixteen

Ilya wanted to stop her. Wanted to throw himself in front of her truck, if necessary. But he could see the pain and determination on Yasmin's face and he knew that nothing and no one could change the way she felt right now. She was furiously angry with him, but more than that, she was bleeding inside, he was sure of it. Because he was hurting inside like he'd never hurt before, too.

Ironic, he thought, as he watched Yasmin's truck disappear up the driveway, that he should only come to realize that he loved his wife in the instant that she left him. He'd fought the feeling, fought the truth, and now it was gone. Self-loathing and remorse engulfed him as he turned and went into the house.

She wouldn't listen to him now, and he could accept that. But it didn't mean he had to remain passive and accept her leaving him. They belonged together. He knew it in his bones. He hadn't wanted to need someone the way he needed her. He shook his head. And here he'd thought losing control was his greatest fear. He'd been a complete and utter fool. Love had been his greatest fear all along. With that, sure, came a loss of control, but he'd finally come to accept that the gift of love far outweighed anything else.

He would get Yasmin back, come hell or high water. Her reaction was understandable. He only hoped that when the dust settled, she'd be prepared to listen to him again.

Yasmin threw herself into work over the next few weeks, refusing to discuss anything with anyone, even Riya, unless it pertained to business. By day she either worked in the office or took the flights on her roster. If there were more flights allocated to them than she'd expected from Horvath Aviation, then that was all well and good, too, although she'd expected the reverse to happen after she left Ilya. The fact that he hadn't canceled their contract had given her pause for thought. Maybe he genuinely had been reaching out to help Carter Air. After all, there were easier routes for him to have taken rather than the convoluted scheme that had raged through her head. But that didn't absolve him from having kept his secret from her. Not at all. The cutting sense of betrayal sliced her anew. All those nights they'd spent together, all the times he could have brought it up…

No, she wouldn't allow herself to think about him. And if she woke up at night with her body screaming for release, her heart breaking and her cheeks wet with tears because she'd been dreaming about him again, then that was just too bad. She'd get over it, just like she'd gotten over every other shitty thing that had ever happened in her life.

Each day there was a text, a telephone message or an email from him. Each day she ruthlessly deleted them. Last night he'd even had the gall to show up at her apartment, knocking on the door and asking her to please talk with him. She'd remained frozen in position on her sofa, staring silently at the door and willing him to leave before she did anything stupid like actually let him in.

No, there would be no further communication between them, unless it was through their lawyers. She didn't need any other reminders of how stupid she'd been to think she'd fallen in love with a man who'd not only witnessed her greatest humiliation, but who'd been party to it. She racked her brain, trying to remember if she'd seen him that night with Jennifer, but the hazy images she could recall all involved Jennifer in queen bee mode, surrounded by her sycophantic sorority sisters.

Which meant that Ilya had to have been in the background. Watching. She shuddered. Whatever his part in that awful night, it no longer mattered. Inasmuch as she could engineer it, he was out of her life. So, too, did *hisgirl* appear to be out of her life. The emails had stopped altogether. Yasmin had followed up with the officer handling her complaint but so far there'd been no new developments. She could only hope that *hisgirl* would leave her alone now that she'd achieved her goal. And on the cop's advice, she'd blocked *hisgirl* from her email.

Yasmin sighed and stared at the proposals piled on her desk. Each one was a pitch for new business. She'd methodically created and reviewed them over and over to make them as sharp and as appealing as they could be. She needed new clients so she could ditch the work that was being provided to her by Horvath.

There was a noise down the hall from her office. Strange, that sounded like a bark, she thought, pushing up from her chair and heading out to see what it was.

"Blaze!" she said, dropping to her knees and accepting an effusive welcome from the puppy who'd managed to slip his leash and come barreling toward her.

"I'm sorry, Yasmin," Riya said as she followed on the puppy's heels. "Ilya dropped him off a minute ago and handed him to me. I couldn't get his leash on him and he knew you were down here. I couldn't stop him once he took off."

"It's okay," Yasmin said, burying her face in the puppy's fur and inhaling the scent of him. "Ilya was here?"

"Only briefly," Riya hastened to tell her. "He asked me to give you this."

She handed Yasmin an envelope. Her first instinct was to tell Riya to take it away and burn it;

she wanted nothing to do with it or the man who'd written it, but in light of the fact that he'd brought Blaze and left him here, she supposed she'd better do the right thing and read it.

"Oh, and he also dropped off Blaze's bed, his crate, his food and bowls."

"He did?"

Yasmin looked from her friend to the puppy in confusion.

"Well, are you going to open his letter?"

"In a minute," Yasmin answered, getting to her feet and giving Blaze a command to sit.

To her surprise, the puppy did exactly as he was told. She gave him a pat and told him he was a good boy before sliding her finger under the flap of the envelope and tearing it open. Her hand shook a little as she extracted the single folded sheet of paper from inside.

"Jeez, Yasmin, the suspense is killing me," Riya commented drily.

Yasmin glared at her friend before unfolding the letter. It contained only one line.

He's pining for you.

She turned the paper over but there was nothing at all on the back.

"So, what did he say?" Riya prompted.

"Here, read it for yourself."

Yasmin thrust the paper at her friend and wondered why on earth the simple missive had left her heart pounding and her stomach doing barrel rolls.

"Hmm," Riya said, pursing her lips. "Not big on words, is he?"

"Not big on anything. Look, if he comes here again just ask him to leave. Okay?"

"If you say so, boss. Do you want me to get one of the boys to take Blaze's things up to your apartment?"

"Thanks, I'd appreciate it."

Yasmin snapped her fingers at the puppy and he followed her into her office where he flopped down on her floor with a happy sigh. She reached into the bottom drawer of her desk for a chew toy she hadn't quite been able to bring herself to throw out. Blaze nosed it then ignored it, instead putting his head on his front paws and closing his eyes.

"Yeah, I wouldn't mind doing that, too," Yasmin said softly.

She tried to turn her focus back to the proposals but her eyes kept drifting to the puppy and her thoughts to the man who'd delivered him here. Why had Ilya given her Blaze? She knew he loved the dog as much as she did. Was this another of his attempts at manipulating her? Did he expect some kind of visitation rights?

"Well," she huffed, making the dog open his eyes and lift his brows a little to look up at her. "One thing's for sure. I'll never know what is going on in that man's mind and I'm better off not knowing anyway."

Ilya picked up the phone in his office, tearing his eyes away from the view of the Carter Air hangar a couple of hundred yards away.

"Yes?" he demanded.

His tone was about as short as his temper lately.

"Hello to you, too," answered his grandmother on the other end of the line. "I see your temperament hasn't improved any since Yasmin left you. I'm beginning to see why she did."

Ilya closed his eyes and swallowed against the retort that sprang to his lips.

"I'm sorry, Nagy," he said in a voice that filtered out all his frustration and tension. "How are you today?"

"I'm tired, my boy."

Ilya sat up a little straighter in his chair. Tired? Nagy never admitted to any physical infirmities, ever.

"Are you all right? Have you been to the doctor?"

She laughed. "Not that sort of tired. I'm tired of how long it's taking you to sort this mess out. I expected more of you, Ilya."

Her censure was a palpable thing through the phone line.

"She's a stubborn woman, Nagy." *Like another woman I know*, he added silently. "I'm working on it."

"Well, work more efficiently. If you really want to prove to her how much she means to you and how much you want her back, you have to understand why she left you in the first place."

"I know why she left me. She thinks I betrayed her trust."

"Then you had better earn it back, hadn't you?"

Before he could answer her, she hung up. He put the phone down on his desk and shook his head.

She was a piece of work, his grandmother. But she was right. These past two weeks he'd been attacking the problem of losing Yasmin head-on, trying to win her back through appeals to her emotions. And she'd blocked him every step of the way. He had to approach this from a different angle.

It would help if he could track down Jennifer and see if his instinct about her involvement in all this was correct, but so far, he had nothing to go on. He didn't have access to any of the pictures or videos that the Hardacres had been sent, and wasn't even entirely clear on how Yasmin had found out about his presence at the hazing that night. Why would Jennifer risk bringing the hazing up again after all these years? She could still get in trouble for that in fact he had every intention of pursuing that angle once he tracked her down. But maybe the trouble had come from someone else who had been there that night.

He forced himself to think logically, to recall exactly what Yasmin had said when he first arrived home from New York.

She'd mentioned emails the morning she walked out. If only he could see them for himself. Then he realized something—Yasmin's laptop had been in the shop for repairs at the time. Sure, she usually checked email on her phone, but there was a chance she could have accessed those emails on his home computer. He could only hope so.

He looked at his day planner. There was nothing today that was so urgent it couldn't be postponed, which meant there was nothing stopping him from going home to find out if Yasmin had used his computer. He got up from his desk, shrugged his suit jacket on and headed for the door.

"Deb, please clear my calendar for the rest of the day," he instructed his assistant as he passed through the outer office.

"Sure thing."

He continued out of the office without breaking his stride and was in the Tesla a few minutes later. He really needed to get that armrest seen to, he thought as he peeled out of the driveway of Horvath Aviation and turned toward Ojai Road. He pushed the speed limit the whole way home. When he got there, he stalked into the house, slamming the double doors behind him. The house was quiet, which meant Hannah had already gone home for the day. He was grateful for that. He had the utmost respect for the housekeeper but he wasn't in the mood for idle chatter right now.

Stripping off his jacket and flinging it to one side, he sat down in his office chair and turned on the computer. He opened the web browser and immediately began to search its history. There. That URL had to be Yasmin's email server, he thought, as a sense of relief vied with the exhilaration of finding something concrete to work with. Of course, she had to have remained logged in to her email account when she closed out of the program if he was going to get any of the information he so desperately sought. He clicked on the link and held his breath.

A massive surge of relief rocked him as her inbox appeared on the screen. Yes, he knew it was an invasion of her privacy to be doing this, but in this case he had to do it. He couldn't fight for her unless he knew what he was fighting against. He scanned the mail marked *read* in her inbox, specifically mail from the night before he'd arrived home.

There were more than fifteen messages from one sender, each with an attachment. He checked them, feeling his ire rise with each and every one. By the time he got to the last one—the photo Jennifer had taken the morning after he'd proposed to her—a red haze of fury blurred his vision. She would pay for this and pay dearly, he silently vowed.

He reached for the phone and called the Horvath Corporation's IT department, asking to be put through to his cousin Sofia. She was a complete computer geek and what she couldn't find out wasn't worth knowing. She was also the soul of discretion. He explained what he needed and allowed her remote access to his computer. He hung up and sat back, watching the cursor race around his screen as she worked her magic.

She called him back a few minutes later.

"You were right. She tried to cover her tracks but she's not as good as she thinks she is. While it took a while to get through the aliases, the activity stems from an account registered to Jennifer Morton."

"Thanks, Sofia. I owe you one."

"I'll add it to the list," she said with a chuckle. "Anything else I can help you with? Tracking Ms. Morton down, perhaps?"

He grimaced at the eagerness in his cousin's voice. No doubt the idea of tracing his ex was far more appealing to her than whatever software issue she was dealing with at Horvath Corporation. "I've got it from here, thanks."

"Okay, then. Well, no doubt I'll see you at the next family wedding."

"Next wedding?"

"Yeah, didn't you hear? Nagy got her claws into Valentin. Seems he was so impressed with the bride she found for you that he said she could find him one, too. He was probably joking but you know Nagy. She isn't going to let it go."

"Strange, he didn't mention anything to me when I saw him the other week," Ilya commented.

But then again, was it so strange? Valentin had always been an intensely private person. Ilya knew he'd been married once before. It was a whirlwind affair that had happened overseas, while he was working on an international medical aid mission. After his return to the States five years ago Valentin had started working with Horvath Pharmaceuticals, mostly out of New York. Ilya wondered if his cousin would be so keen to enter into another marriage if he knew the mess Ilya had made of his own. So far Ilya had kept the news of his separation from his wife between himself and Alice, whom he'd sworn to secrecy, because he refused to believe he couldn't win Yasmin back.

Now, hopefully, with the information Sofia had given him, no one else in the family would ever need to find out, because he planned to find Jennifer Morton and do what he should have done years ago.

"Yeah, well, you know Valentin," Sofia said, interrupting his thoughts. "All I can say is Galen had better keep his wits about him. If he isn't careful, Nagy will be clipping his playboy ways next."

Ilya forced a laugh. "Then you'd be next if we're going in birth order," he warned.

"Let's not go there," Sofia said hastily. "Well, if there's nothing else…?"

He knew that once he turned the conversation to her private life, she'd end their call.

"No, but thanks again."

When Ilya hung up, he made a note to send her a case of her favorite wine. Then he turned his attention to tracking Jen down. With today's social media, how hard could it be, right?

Harder than he thought, he discovered. If she had any social media accounts she kept them very private. Ilya found himself looking up several old acquaintances to track her down. He was on the verge of giving up and calling in a private investigator when one of her sorority sisters replied to his private message, gushing about how excited Jen would be to hear from him again.

Apparently his ex was living in a trailer park outside of Las Vegas. He looked at his watch. It was a two-hour flight to Vegas. Plotting the flight plan in his head he figured he could be there before dark.

In the next instant he was on his feet and heading back out to the car. It was time to put a stop to Jen's cruelty once and for all, and win Yasmin back in the process.

Seventeen

He pulled his rental to a stop outside a single-wide trailer that stood out from its neighbors due to its obvious signs of neglect. The paint was peeling, weeds were growing all over the lot and one of the windows was broken and covered with a piece of cardboard. But he didn't waste a moment getting out the car and going to knock on the door.

"Well, hello there, handsome," Jen said as she opened the door. The sour smell of alcohol wafted off her. It was overpowering and turned his stomach.

He looked at her in shock. The years hadn't been kind, but then, neither had she, so he couldn't be entirely surprised. She still wore her hair the same way, but it was uncombed and looked like it hadn't seen shampoo in several days. Her skin held a dingy tone.

And she was unmistakably drunk, or high, or both. But he wasn't here to enquire about her welfare.

"Why did you do it?" he asked straight out.

"I'm fine, thank you. And you?" she answered with a sly smile. "It's been a while."

"Let's not beat around the bush, Jen. Why did you do it? Why hurt Yasmin more than you already did?"

She met his eyes and for a second he thought he saw a flicker of bravado there. But then she averted her gaze, her entire body sagging in surrender.

"You'd better come in," she said sullenly.

He couldn't think of anything he'd rather do less, but if he was to get the answers he needed he'd have to accept her less than gracious invitation.

"Take a seat," she said, gesturing to a sagging couch strewn with tabloid magazines and newspapers. The coffee table was covered in empty wine bottles and dirty glasses.

"No, thank you. I'll stand."

Jen reached for a packet of cigarettes and put one in her mouth, lighting it with shaking hand. She took a long draw and blew out a steady stream of smoke, obviously in no rush to talk. Clearly she needed a reminder as to why he was here.

"I know you're behind the emails. What I don't know is why."

She shrugged and took another drag on her cigarette. "She deserved it."

"I beg your pardon?" His voice was icy cold.

"Why should she have you when I couldn't? Living the high life when all I have is this," she said, vaguely gesturing toward the room. "I saw the write-up about your wedding in one of these magazines. To be honest, when I heard you'd married her I couldn't believe it. Her, of all people. She was the reason you left me. I don't see why she gets to have you in the end. It pissed me off. So I sent her a little message. No crime in that."

He couldn't believe what he was hearing. She was obviously in an altered state, but her hatred had a cold, hard logic to it. "What you did was threatening and a criminal nuisance."

She looked at him again; this time he saw fear in her eyes. "You can't prove anything."

"I can, Jen. It's easy to prove those emails to Yasmin and the Hardacres came from you. It's how I found you."

She'd been a clever woman in college. How on earth had she come to this?

"So, you found me. What are you going to do with me now? I can think of a few things." She ground out her half-smoked cigarette, took a step closer to him and reached out a hand to touch him. "We used to be so good together. We can be again."

Ilya fought down the bile that rose in his throat. He wrapped his fingers around her wrist and very deliberately removed her hand from his body.

"That is never going to happen."

"What a shame," she said with a flippant toss of her head.

"You're going to face charges for this."

"Oh, says who?"

"Me. I've already lodged a complaint with my local police and forwarded them all the emails you sent to my wife." He placed special emphasis on the last two words. "I also contacted the Hardacres. They're co-operating with the investigation, too."

"Always the upstanding citizen, aren't you?" she sneered.

"Look, I let you get away with bullying Yasmin once before. I'm not doing it again. The way I see it, we can do this the hard way or the easy way."

"I always liked it hard," she said with a sleazy smile. He ignored her, wondering what he'd ever seen in her in the first place.

"Look, one way or the other you're going to face charges, but if you want leniency, you'll need to co-operate with me. It's is entirely up to you."

She sniffed and reached for another cigarette. "So what's in it for me? What is it that you expect me to do?"

"For a start, you will send a written apology to my wife for your recent and past actions. You will also explain to Esme Hardacre, in person, why you sabotaged my wife's contract."

"And if I don't?"

"I'll make sure you face the full weight of the law and I'll ask the police to file additional charges against you for the hazing incident while we're at it. Thanks to the photos you sent to Yasmin, I'm fairly sure we can make a pretty good case."

"You stuck-up bastard. You don't leave me any choice, do you? Fine, I'll do it. Although leaving all this behind is going to be such hardship."

He couldn't stand to be in the trailer with her a moment longer and went to wait outside while she gathered a few of her things together. It wasn't until they were in the plane and headed back toward California that he began to hope that maybe, just maybe, he might be able to earn his wife back.

Yasmin had had Blaze back for a whole week and was grateful for the company. He listened—while she raged and while she wept. Without judgment, without censure, without advice. And she was getting there—recovering from the emotional strain of the last few weeks. Not quite out of the woods yet, but stronger every day.

None of it stopped her missing Ilya, though. Her longing for him was a deep physical ache and she continued to throw herself into long hours at work in between exercising Blaze and seeing to it he had sufficient socialization time at a new doggy day care closer to the airport. He was there today and she kept checking the clock, aware his pickup time was looming.

There was a knock at her office door. Yasmin looked up from her desk, grateful for the interruption. It seemed she spent more time at her desk than flying aircraft these days.

"What is it, Riya?" she asked her friend, who hovered in the doorway with a look of uncertainty on her face.

"Esme Hardacre's here to see you. She says it's very important."

Yasmin's heart skipped beat. "She's here to see me?"

"Oh, yes."

Yasmin took a minute to tidy up the papers spread everywhere and quickly checked her appearance in the small mirror she kept behind the door. She rarely wore makeup but she should at least slick a little color onto her lips. She dabbed on some of the tinted gloss she kept in her top drawer and shoved her fingers through her short hair, giving it a touch more lift, then straightened her shoulders.

"Please show her in," Yasmin finally said, taking a deep breath. It was time to see what Esme Hardacre wanted.

Eighteen

By the time Yasmin let herself and Blaze into the apartment later that evening she was exhausted. The meeting with Esme Hardacre had been both awkward and intriguing. Most surprising of all: Esme had come to apologize. Long story short, Jennifer Morton had shown up at Esme's office and admitted to sending Hardacre Incorporated the damning photos and had confessed they were out of context.

According to Esme, Ilya had tracked Jennifer down, taken her to Esme, and when their conversation was finished, turned her over to the police.

Esme was truly sorry that she and her husband had assumed Yasmin was at fault. She'd asked Yasmin if she would consider signing a new contract with them on revised terms. The ball was now in Yasmin's court.

She'd wanted to tell Esme Hardacre exactly what she could do with her offer; that had been her knee-jerk reaction. But reason had prevailed. In the end, Yasmin had asked for a few days to consider things, and that was where they'd left it.

Could she do business with someone who'd seen the evidence of the degradation she'd suffered? Would she see censure, or worse, pity, in their eyes every time she saw them again? Her thoughts tumbled round in her mind, over and over. Fiscally it made excellent sense to agree to renegotiate terms and she had to admit to a certain grudging respect for the woman who'd shown up in person to make her apology. Logically there was no room for emotion in all of this. Maybe it really was time to stop allowing that night to define the rest of her life.

Then, as she was showing Esme out, a courier had arrived with an envelope addressed to her. Inside was a letter with "I'm sorry" for a subject line and a detailed apology. The letter was signed by Jennifer Morton. A raft of emotions assailed Yasmin, but through it all was an immense sense of relief that Jennifer's malicious mischief was over.

While Yasmin reheated the takeout she'd bought the night before, she fed Blaze his evening meal. It was only after she'd eaten, and had taken Blaze out for a toilet stop, that she accepted that she'd allowed herself to be a victim for far too long.

Yes, she'd forged on with her grandfather's company. Yes, she'd fulfilled both his and many of her own dreams along the way. But all along, she'd given

Jennifer far more power and sway over her life than she ever should have. She'd allowed what had happened to her to color everything she did from that night on.

Yes, it had been shocking, but by holding on to it, by nurturing the fear, she'd only made it worse. She'd thought she'd worked through it all, but she hadn't. She'd only worked around it, never actually facing what had happened to her head-on. Reading Jennifer's humble apology today—in which she'd mentioned that Ilya had tracked her down and made her come clean—had ripped the blinkers from her eyes. Jennifer wasn't an ogre to fear and resent. She was her own kind of mixed-up and messed-up human being. And now it was time for Yasmin to shed the past and take back control of her life.

But where to begin? With the Hardacre contract? With Ilya?

Just thinking about her husband made every internal muscle in her body seize up with longing so intense it brought tears to her eyes. It was only when she felt the swish of Blaze's feathered puppy tail against the back of her leg that she blinked her eyes clear and forced herself back to the here and now.

"C'mon, boy. Let's get back upstairs."

He'd become surprisingly agile on the stairs, even in the week she'd had him. It amazed her how quickly he'd grown and how much he'd changed since she and Ilya had found him on the trail that day. Was it only six weeks ago? She swallowed against the lump of emotion in her throat. So much had changed in that time.

Could she even begin to hope that she and Ilya could patch things up? Did she dare trust him again? No matter what he'd done since she left him in tracking Jennifer down and forcing her to face her behavior, he had still deliberately withheld the truth of his involvement in that night. Jennifer's letter had said he was not a part of the hazing and that he'd only arrived at the beach at the end. But he had been there. So, how had he been involved?

Blaze trotted through to her bedroom, and she heard him settle on his bed with a contented sigh. She switched on the television and desultorily flicked through the channels, not finding anything that held her attention longer than two minutes. In the end she switched the TV off and stared at the blank screen.

Was it an analogy for her future? she wondered. A blank canvas waiting to be written? She started at a knock on her apartment door. She flicked a look at the time on her watch. It was late for someone to come calling. She opened the door.

"Alice?"

The older lady swept past her into the open-plan living–dining area of the apartment and looked around.

"It's as though your grandfather still lives here," she commented with a haughty tone.

"Thank you, I like the decor, too."

Alice sniffed, clearly not a fan. "He always was a minimalist—in life as well as in love."

"That's hardly fair. He loved you with his dying breath," Yasmin snapped back. At the stricken look on Alice's face, she reined in her temper. "I'm sorry. That was uncalled for. I've had a rather trying day and I took my frustration out on you. I shouldn't have."

Alice rubbed her chest a moment before nodding gently. "No, it was called for. I apologize."

Yasmin sighed internally. Apparently it was a day for apologies and unexpected visitations. "Would you like to sit down?"

Alice moved to the only easy chair in the room while Yasmin resumed her position on the couch. From Yasmin's bedroom, Blaze bounded across the floor and sniffed at the newcomer.

"So this is the puppy?"

"His name is Blaze."

Yasmin wondered why Alice was here. She was a little breathless. Whether it was because of the climb up the stairs that led to the apartment or because she didn't like the dog, Yasmin wasn't sure.

"Are you okay with him here? I can put him back in my room if you'd like."

"No, no. He's fine."

Alice looked around the room again, her eyes alighting on one of the photos of Yasmin's grandfather. The older woman rose gracefully to her feet and walked over to the frame, lifting it up and looking at it more closely.

"Such a handsome man and such a clever engineer," she said in a faraway voice. "And he could dance better than any man I knew."

Yasmin looked at her in surprise. "Granddad? Dance?"

A soft smile curved Alice's lips. "Oh, yes, he was quite the dancer back in the day." She set the photo down and turned to face Yasmin. "I loved him very much, you know."

"But not enough to marry him, apparently." Yasmin found it hard to keep the bitterness from her voice.

"He never asked me."

Yasmin looked at her in shock. "But you knew he loved you."

"*Suspected* it, yes. And I loved him in return. But I also loved Eduard." Her voice broke a little and Alice took in a deep breath. "You have no idea how hard it was, loving two men. Men who had always been friends, whose friendly rivalry turned into a fierce competition over me. Sometimes I think it would have been better if my father had never taken us from Hungary and brought us here to America. But then I would never have had my family, never have built our dynasty."

"How did you choose between Granddad and Eduard?"

"In the end it came down to one thing. Eduard was the man who *told* me he loved me. He was the one who asked me to marry him. I was a bit of a silly young thing then, lost in the romance of being pursued by two handsome men without considering the consequences of what would happen next when I chose one over the other.

"Don't get me wrong. I don't regret my decision,

but I'm truly sorry for the unhappiness that I caused Jim. I'm sorry for how it impacted on the relationship he had with the woman he eventually married and on his relationship with your father and you."

Yasmin didn't know where to look or what to say. Alice walked back to her chair and sat down again. Silence stretched between them until Alice spoke again.

"Do you love my grandson, Yasmin?"

"I beg your pardon?"

"It's quite simple really. Do you love Ilya?"

"No, it's not simple. He betrayed me. I can't trust him anymore."

"Did you know he was the person who swam out to you the night of your hazing? He saved your life."

"How did you—?"

"Oh, I have my ways," Alice said with a wave of slender, wrinkled hand. "I'm a firm believer in fate, my dear. There was a reason he was there that night, and it wasn't because he was a party to what that evil girl did to you. He was there for a far higher purpose."

"I didn't know. He didn't tell me."

"Did you give him a chance?"

The question hung on the air like an unwelcome guest in the room. Yasmin shook her head.

"No, to be brutally honest, I didn't give him a chance."

"Nor would I under similar circumstances," Alice acceded with a sad smile. "There's a lot my grandson doesn't share—with me or with anyone else. He is fierce and loyal, but careful, too. He's a good man. An honest one. But he doesn't give his love easily. Nor do you. My dear, you need to decide if your love for Ilya is worth putting aside your past hurts."

"I didn't say I loved him," Yasmin answered with all the stubbornness she'd inherited from her grandfather. It was an instinctive reaction, one that came from a place of self-protection.

Alice simply smiled at her, understanding clear in her eyes. "You're a lot like Jim, but you have your father's sensitivity, too. I think that if you and Ilya can weather this, and overcome it, you will be an unbreakable force together in the future. But you have to want it—and you have to fight for it if you do want it."

"I don't even know if he loves me. He's never said as much."

"No, he isn't the kind of man who wears his heart on his sleeve. He used to be, but, like you, he was hurt. Are you willing to risk the rest of your life not knowing what the two of you could have had together? Are his past transgressions so bad that you can't forgive him and move on?"

Yasmin let the words sink deeply into her heart. She'd barely let Ilya get a word in that day she'd left him. She'd still been filled with all the shock and hurt and confusion at the news he'd been engaged to Jennifer Morton. And now she knew he'd been the one who actually dragged her from the water and prevented her from drowning. Had she misjudged him so badly?

She thought about what he'd done since she left him. Giving her Blaze, hunting down Jennifer, pressing charges and making the other woman apologize—not only to her but the Hardacres, as well. And then there was what he'd done to help her hold on to Carter Air, sending Horvath Aviation business her way. Giving her the funds to repay her loan. She hadn't asked for any of it, and yet he'd done all those things *for her.*

At the very least, she owed him a hearing.

"Well," Alice said, rising to her feet again. "I have said what I came here to say. I hope to see you again soon, my dear."

"Thank you for coming," Yasmin said automatically as she saw Alice to the door. "I mean it. It's been a difficult time."

"Life's never easy, but it is what you make of it."

Yasmin closed the door behind Alice and leaned against it, letting Ilya's grandmother's words filter through her racing mind. Could she make it? Could they? Did it matter so very much that Ilya hadn't told her the whole truth and if it did, could she forgive him?

There was only one way to find out.

Nineteen

"Come on, Blaze. We're going for a ride."

The puppy bounded toward her, tongue lolling in his mouth and his eyes bright with excitement at the word.

She took her time driving to Ilya's hillside home, wondering all the way whether or not she should have called ahead first, at least to see if he was home. But it didn't matter now; she was committed to seeing this through. Weariness pulled at her whole body. It had been a heck of a day so far and it didn't look like it was letting up any time soon.

Next to her, harnessed in his special seat belt, Blaze got excited as she pulled up outside the gate to the house. She'd left her auto opener behind, believing she'd never need it again. She hesitated, debating whether to turn around and head back to the airfield or to press the buzzer and ask for admittance.

The gates ahead of her slowly rolled aside. That meant one of two things. Either Ilya was on his way out, or he'd seen her on the security camera and opened the gate himself.

She put the truck in gear and started her descent down the driveway. She passed the helipad, noting that one of the choppers from the Horvath fleet was there. Was Ilya planning on heading out somewhere? Or did he have visitors? Her hands were shaking as she pulled up outside the front of the house. Ilya was framed in the doorway.

Her heart all but beat itself out of her chest the moment she saw him there. Tall, strong and so handsome there should be a law against it. And so dear to her fragile heart that she barely knew what to do or say anymore. Beside her, Blaze gave a happy woof of recognition. She unclipped his harness and leaned across the door to open it and let him bound out.

Ilya bent to welcome the puppy, who wriggled and yipped and licked with all the joy and exuberance of a puppy who'd been parted from a loved one for months or years rather than days.

"Are you getting out?" Ilya asked, looking up at her across the bench seat of the truck. "Or were you just dropping him off for a visit?"

A surge of anger filled her. How dare he be flippant at a time like this? She fought the urge to pull the door closed, put the truck in gear and head back up the driveway. Didn't he know how difficult this was for her?

How could he, a voice deep inside her asked, *when you won't even talk to him?*

Yasmin released the breath she was holding and forced herself to get down from the truck. She walked toward Ilya, feeling distinctly lightheaded while at the same time feeling as though the weight of her future, both hers and Ilya's, hung around her shoulders like a leaden cloak.

"Do you want to come in?" Ilya offered, standing up.

"I think that's best," she managed, her voice sounding stiff and unnatural to her own ears.

She walked through to the family room off the kitchen and stood at the sliding doors looking out to the patio. Blaze scratched at the glass, desperate to get outside and hunt out a play toy. She let him through and followed him outside.

"Can I get you anything?" Ilya asked from behind her.

"Some courage perhaps?" she answered wryly.

"Courage? Oh, I don't know. I kind of think you're one of the bravest women I know."

"I don't deserve that."

"What makes you think that?"

"At the first sign of trouble, I run."

"Self-preservation. There's probably many an extinct species that wishes they'd perfected the art of running."

She smiled at his attempt at humor.

"I had a visitor or two today," she said. "And received a letter by special delivery."

"Ah, yes." Ilya nodded and looked across the patio to where Blaze was happily sniffing his way around the edge of the garden. "Shall we sit down and talk about that?"

She took a seat at the large granite outdoor table and rested her arms on the surface. The warmth of the sun still emanated from the smooth rock and she took strength from it.

"Did you always know?" she blurted out.

"Know?" Ilya looked directly at her.

"That it was me you saved from drowning."

"No. Absolutely not. Not until the day we went up in the Ryan. When we talked, after…y'know."

His eyes flared a deeper blue. She felt an answering curl of heat deep inside at the memory.

"Why didn't you say anything?"

"I couldn't. You'd just shared your worst experience with me. Telling you about my part in it right then would have compounded what was already a terrible memory. After that, well, everything unraveled around us so quickly after that. I know it's my fault and I shouldn't make excuses, but I didn't want to risk damaging the tentative relationship we were building."

"Shouldn't relationships be built on trust?"

He nodded and looked away briefly before turning his attention back to her. "They should, and I will always regret that I didn't tell you sooner. That you had to find out the way you did. But I can't undo the past. I'm always going to be linked to the worst thing in your life.

"When I got there, you were just entering the water. I could see you were already in a bad way. I asked Jen what she was thinking, letting you swim in that state, but she said you wanted to. I watched you, saw the moment your arms looked like they were getting too heavy for you, when you started to sink. I went after you and brought you back to the beach."

"Thank you. I never knew who pulled me out, never got the chance to say thanks."

"It was what any decent person would have done. Unfortunately, decent people were thin on the sand that night."

There was an undercurrent of fury in his voice, as if the whole episode still made him incredibly angry. Judging from his fists clenched on the table, it probably did.

"And you got Jennifer to apologize to me?"

"I did."

"I'd begun to suspect her, but when were you sure it was her?"

He scrubbed a hand over his face. "The first couple of weeks you were gone I didn't know what to do—you kept rebuffing me at every turn so I had to find another way. I remembered you saying something about emails."

He explained how he'd checked his home computer, apologizing for invading her private email, and told her how he'd asked his cousin for help in tracking down where the threatening emails had come from.

“So you went all bounty hunter on her? Even the police didn’t uncover all that,” Yasmin said incredulously.

“They probably didn’t see the urgency like I did. I had a lot more riding on it. I had to prove to you that I wasn’t who you thought I was. You needed to know who was behind that whole thing and you needed compensation for that.”

He explained how he’d turned Jennifer over to the police and the charges she was facing. It was something that the police would be in touch with Yasmin about. But he also mentioned how Jennifer clearly had an addiction problem, and she’d come willingly to apologize to the Hardacres and written the letter to Yasmin essentially admitting her guilt. He hinted that with Yasmin’s agreement, Jennifer may be eligible for treatment for her addictions in lieu of serious jailtime. As he spoke Yasmin realized just what a special person he was.

“Well, I’m glad you did all that. It allowed me to close a door on the past. By the way, Esme Hardacre stopped by today.”

He looked at her, waiting for her to say more. “And?”

“She wants to renegotiate our contract. I said I’d think about it.”

“If you do that, you won’t need my help any longer.”

Something in his voice made him sound lost. As if he thought that without the work he was putting her way, she wouldn’t need him anymore.

“Do you want me to need your help?”

He swallowed. "Not my help. To be totally honest with you, Yasmin, I want you to need me the way I need you. I love you."

Yasmin's eyes widened into giant slate-gray pools. Was it fear, rejection or hope that he saw reflected there? He prayed it was the latter. He'd done everything he could to make this right, everything in his power. Leaving it in her hands now was the hardest thing he'd ever done. Harder than landing a plane knowing that there was nothing that could be done for his father. Harder than standing at his mother's grave and knowing that he hadn't been enough to fill her life and keep her safe. Harder than admitting he'd been a poor judge of character when he'd chosen Jennifer to be his future bride.

But Yasmin was a chance at a future he'd never expected. A future he now wanted with his heart and soul. He'd move heaven and earth if she asked for it. But she wasn't the kind of person to ask for anything. She was self-sufficient. An island. How did a man get across that sea of independence she surrounded herself with? How did he get her to understand how very much she meant to him, especially when he'd only just begun to understand it himself?

Yasmin's voice was hesitant when she spoke. "Needing someone else scares me. It makes me feel less worthy. Certainly, less worthy of love."

Ilya shook his head fiercely. "Never less worthy of love. You are an incredible woman. You've done so much. You never give up."

"I gave up on us."

"Extenuating circumstances." He rushed to absolve her of any guilt.

"No, Ilya, I need to own this, the same way I need to own the fact that I let Jennifer—all the Jennifers of this world—drive my decisions and my idea of my own worth for far too long. The thing is, it wasn't until I married you that I actually started to learn what love really was."

Ilya let her words sink in, felt the burning spark of hope flicker to life in his chest.

She continued. "You weren't what I expected at all. You have to realize, I was conditioned to hate you on sight."

"I got that impression when you ran away from our wedding ceremony."

"Not my finest moment and, again, one driven by fear. I don't want fear to rule my life anymore, Ilya. I want to be in control."

How could she not see that she was already in control? That she'd always been. Didn't she understand that a weaker person could have been completely broken by what happened to her—from her parents abandoning her to a grumpy old man, to constantly trying to win his approval, to being the outsider even when she was at college? Each piece on its own was enough, but she'd dealt with all of that. He told her as much.

"Thank you for the compliments. It's not often I get to see myself through someone else's eyes."

Blaze abandoned his circuit of the garden and came and sat on the patio between them, a contented little sigh coming from him before he put his head down and drifted off to sleep. Ilya looked at the puppy and, for a moment, envied him the simplicity of his life. But then, if Ilya's life were that simple he wouldn't have this beautiful, strong, complicated woman sitting opposite him. A woman who held his heart in her capable hands.

"I meant every one of them, just as I meant it when I said I love you. I know I let you down by not telling you the truth about me and Jen. I regret that more than I can say. Your trust is important to me, Yasmin. It's everything. Without it I feel like I'm only half a person. You are my other half. Will you forgive me my silence? Will you give us, give *me* a second chance?"

"Ilya, I came here tonight not really knowing what I wanted to say. Trust is the biggest thing for me and I did feel betrayed by you. But my perception of that night, of your part in it, was warped—just like my perception of you when I saw you standing at the altar was warped by all the hideous things my grandfather used to say about your family." She took a deep breath and reached across the table to grip his hands. "I don't want to work against you anymore. I want to work with you. To be honest, I don't want to accept the Hardacre contract. I want to work with you, properly, the way our grandfathers started to, the way they should have continued to. If you're willing.

"I'm not going to let what other people say or said, or do or did, stand in the way of my happiness any longer. I'm the one who makes my decisions, my choices, and I choose you. For far too long I strove to find where I fit in this world. I didn't fit with my mom and dad, and I never truly fit with Granddad, either. At school I was that kid who won the prizes but who no one wanted to sit with at lunch. At college, well…" She shrugged and took a deep breath. "I never felt like I fit anywhere, but I know where I want to belong. Here, with you. I love you, Ilya, and I want to tell you that every day for the rest of our lives. They're not words that come easily to me, nor am I used to hearing them. I never thought I needed them, but I do. Can we try again? Can we make our marriage work?"

Ilya was out of his chair and pulling her into his arms before she even finished talking.

"I will tell you every minute of every day for the rest of my life how much you mean to me. I might not always use the exact words, but you will never need to doubt me or my love for you, ever again," he vowed.

She looked up at him, her hands bracketing his face. "I'm going to need help on this one, on understanding what it takes to be a part of a couple, on learning that I don't have to stand on my own two feet on every issue, every single day. I'll need help to learn how to open up to you, to be worthy of your love, too."

"I'm here for you, always. No more secrets."

"No more secrets," she repeated softly.

Ilya kissed her, his lips sealing a promise that transcended words and he knew, in his heart of hearts, that they'd work everything out together. And, as he removed her wedding ring from his pocket, where he put it each day, and replaced it on her finger, he knew they'd get there. Maybe not today, maybe not tomorrow, but they had the future. A long, long future.

Together.

* * * * *

If you loved this novel of sizzling drama,
pick up these other books from
USA TODAY *bestselling author Yvonne Lindsay!*

LITTLE SECRETS: THE BABY MERGER
ONE HEIR... OR TWO?
CONTRACT WEDDING, EXPECTANT BRIDE
ARRANGED MARRIAGE, BEDROOM SECRETS
WANTING WHAT SHE CAN'T HAVE

Available now from Harlequin Desire!

***

If you're on Twitter, tell us what you think of
Harlequin Desire! #harlequindesire

COMING NEXT MONTH FROM

Available July 3, 2018

#2599 SECRET TWINS FOR THE TEXAN

Texas Cattleman's Club: The Impostor • by Karen Booth

Dani left town after the rancher broke her heart, but now she's back... with twin boys who look just like him! Given his secrets, he knows better than to fall in love, but their chemistry can't be denied. Will the truth destroy everything?

#2600 THE FORBIDDEN BROTHER

The McNeill Magnates • by Joanne Rock

Reclusive rancher Cody McNeill refuses to let photographer Jillian Ross onto his land, but then a chance encounter at a bar leads to an explosive night. Now he can't let her go—even after he learns that she meant to seduce his twin brother!

#2601 THE RANCHER'S HEIR

Billionaires and Babies • by Sara Orwig

Wealthy rancher Noah Grant has returned to Texas to fulfill a promise, but what he finds is the woman he once loved hiding the baby he's never known. Can he and Camilla overcome what tore them apart and find a way to forever?

#2602 HIS ENEMY'S DAUGHTER

First Family of Rodeo • by Sarah M. Anderson

Pete Wellington's father lost the family rodeo business in a poker game years ago. The owner's beautiful daughter, Chloe, holds the reins now, so it's time to go undercover and steal it back! But what happens if the sexy businesswoman steals his heart instead?

#2603 FRIENDSHIP ON FIRE

Love in Boston • by Joss Wood

Jules wrote off her former best friend when he left years ago. Now he's back...and demanding she pretend to be his fiancée to protect his business! She agrees to help, but that's only because she wants to take it from fake to forever...

#2604 ON TEMPORARY TERMS

Highland Heroes • by Janice Maynard

Lawyer Abby Hartman is falling hard for wealthy Scotsman Duncan Stewart, but when she learns his present is tied to a secret from her past, can she prove her innocence and convince him what they share is real?

YOU CAN FIND MORE INFORMATION ON UPCOMING HARLEQUIN® TITLES, FREE EXCERPTS AND MORE AT WWW.HARLEQUIN.COM.

HDCNM0618

SPECIAL EXCERPT FROM

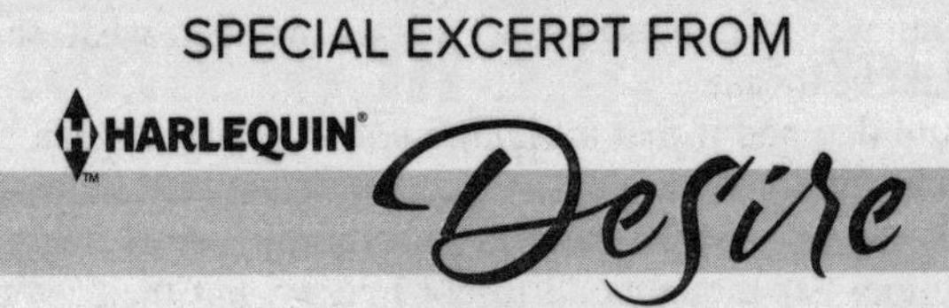

Reclusive rancher Cody McNeill refuses to let photographer Jillian Ross onto his land, but then a chance encounter at a bar leads to an explosive night. Now he can't let her go—even after he learns that she meant to seduce his twin brother!

Read on for a sneak peek of THE FORBIDDEN BROTHER by Joanne Rock, part of her ***McNEILL MAGNATES*** *series!*

Cody McNeill knew—instantly—that the lovely redhead seated in the booth across the way had mistaken him for his twin.

His whole life, he'd witnessed women stare at Carson in just that manner—like he was the answer to all their fantasies. It was strange, really, since he and Carson were supposedly identical. To people who knew them, they couldn't be more different. Even strangers could usually tell at a glance that Carson was the charmer and Cody was…not.

But somehow the redhead hadn't quite figured it out yet.

Between the dark mood hovering over Cody and the realization that he wouldn't mind stealing away one of his brother's admirers, he did something he hadn't done since he was a schoolkid.

He pretended to be his twin.

"Would you like some tips on what's edible around here?" He tested out the words with a smile.

"Edible?"

"On the menu," he clarified. "There are some good options if you'd like input."

The way she blushed, he had to wonder what she'd thought he meant.

And damned if that intriguing notion didn't distract him from his dark mood.

"I, um..." She bit her lip uncertainly before seeming to collect her thoughts. "I'm not hungry, but thank you. I actually followed you in here to speak to you."

Ah, hell. He wasn't ready to end the game that had taken a turn for the interesting. But it was one thing to ride the wave of the woman's mistaken assumption. It was another to lie, and Cody's ethics weren't going to allow him to sink that low.

The smile his brother normally wore slid from Cody's face. Disappointment cooled the heat in his veins.

The music in the bar switched to a slow tempo that gave him an idea for putting off a conversation he didn't care to have.

"Are you sure you want to talk?" Shoving himself to his feet, he extended a hand to her. "We could dance instead."

He stared down into those green-gold eyes, willing her to say yes. But then, surprise of all surprises, the sweetest smile curved her lips, transforming her face from pretty to...

Wow.

"That sounds great," she agreed with a breathless laugh. "Thank you."

Sliding her cool fingers into his palm, she rose and let him lead her to the dance floor.

HDEXP0618